Call on the Wind

Call on the Wind

David Donald

First published by Jacana Media (Pty) Ltd in 2007

10 Orange Street
Sunnyside
Auckland Park 2092
South Africa
+2711 628 3200
www.jacana.co.za

© David Donald, 2007

All rights reserved.

ISBN   978-1-77009-360-7

Cover design by miss sweden
Artwork by Jiggs Snaddon
Set in Sabon 11.5/14pt
Printed by CTP Books, Cape Town
Job No. 000451

See a complete list of Jacana titles at www.jacana.co.za

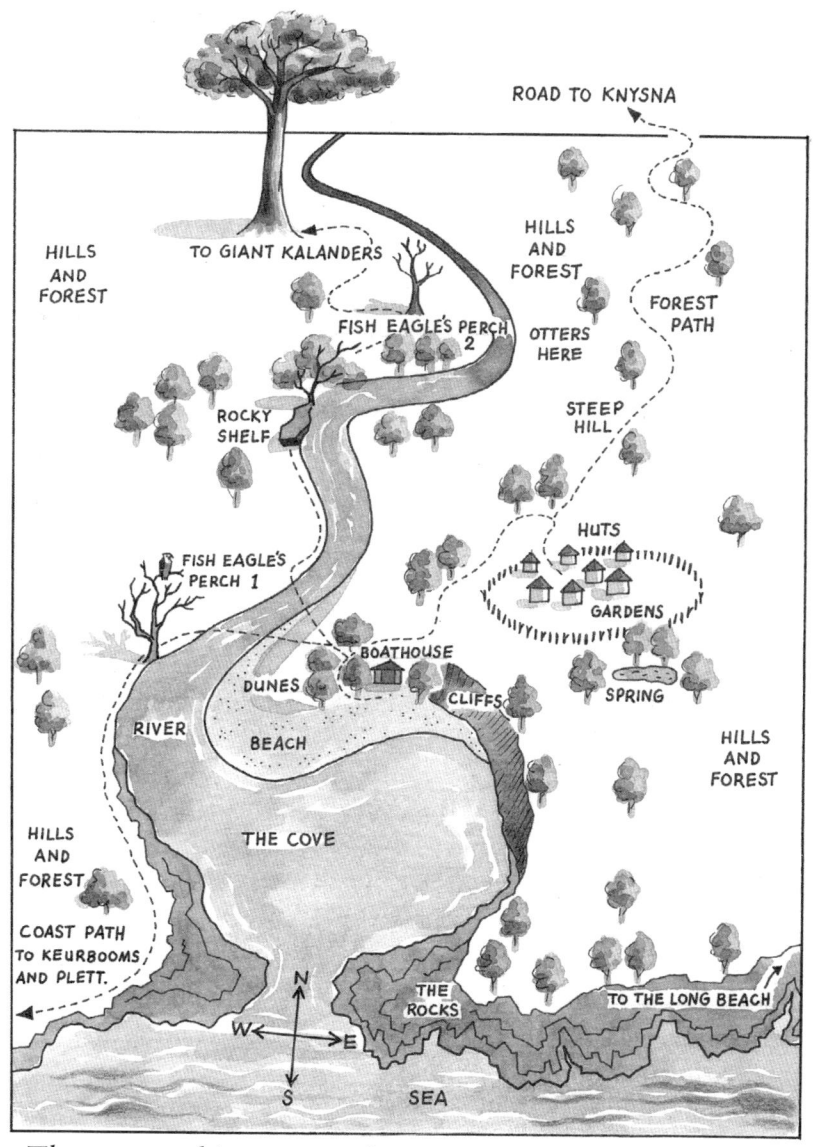

The cove and its surroundings

Acknowledgments

Thanks to Chief Samuel Jansen of the Kranshoek Griqua community, for valuable oral historical information; and to Don Pinnock, Jan Esterhuyse, Brian Snaddon, Jenny Hatton and members of my family, all of whose input and thoughtful comments have been so helpful in the writing of this story.

Contents

1. What the Fish Eagle Knew — 9
2. The Ache in Isaak's Heart — 20
3. The Song in the Guitar — 29
4. A Flash of Silver — 35
5. A Gift Sent From the Sea — 44
6. Die Vissers' Lied — 52
7. Lied van die Bos — 61
8. A Fishing Rod and a Dress — 68
9. Harmonies over the Cove — 77
10. A Dream and a Water Dance — 83
11. The Dark Cloud — 91
12. The Skipper's Tiller — 101
13. The Cloud Lightens — 105
14. The Call of the Fish Eagle — 111

Postscript — *118*
Glossary of Afrikaans and Colloquial Language — *120*

Chapter One

What the Fish Eagle Knew

"Isaak, load up the lines... also put the net in today," called his father. "Opskud! Opskud nou!" Isaak stood with a bundle of hand lines near the boat. He stared out to sea and took a deep breath. The morning was calm and clear. An off-shore breeze blew lightly from behind him. Gleaming in the dawn light, slow, heaving swells rolled gently into the sheltered circle of the cove.

The signs were all right: it was a perfect morning to be going out. The fishing would be good today. He just knew it. But then, to be really sure, he remembered that he should also check the fish eagle.

His father had always said to him, "First thing in the morning, you must always look carefully at the sea, the wind and the sky. There've been many storms at the cove. You know that, Isaak. We've got to be sure that it'll be safe to take the boat out to sea."

So Isaak understood that you had to look at the waves. The swells should be coming in slow, straight lines right into the cove. They should not be criss-crossing or, worse still, marching in at an angle and crashing angrily into the rocks at the narrow entrance. You also had to note the wind. If it was blowing gently off-shore in the morning, that was usually a good sign. But if it was gusting from the west or further to the north, that was often bad news. More than this, the wind sometimes moved differently, high in the sky, to the way it blew on the ground. The clouds could tell you a lot about this. Low, puffy clouds were usually fine. But high, streaky clouds stretching across from the north-west, even if it was calm below, were often a sign that bad weather was on its way.

Apart from these signs, Isaak had also learned to watch the fish eagle in the early morning. If the weather was going to be good, he'd see it sitting on the top branch of a dead tree near the cove: it liked to catch fish where the river flowed into the sea. But, if stormy weather was on its way, he'd see it perched on a tall tree deep in the forest and far up the river. It seemed to know that the weather was changing.

The other men laughed at Isaak and his fish eagle story.

"Ag, Isaak, dis sommer twak!" they said. "A bird can't tell you if bad weather's coming. You can only know by the sea, the wind and the clouds."

Isaak understood that these weather signs were important, so he didn't argue. But he still kept a look-out for the fish eagle. He believed that it knew something that they didn't.

On this morning, the fish eagle was right there, perched on its favourite tree near the cove. Isaak smiled up at it, and then bent his back into folding and loading the net into the boat.

By this time the others were around the boat house, helping to get the boat ready, some stowing the bait, others getting the sail ready and checking the rigging. There were seven men in the crew. His father was the captain – or 'skipper', as they called him. He was the oldest and most experienced man on the boat. His face was weathered and wrinkled by the sun, his body as tough as biltong, and his eyes bright and alert. He was strict with his crew, as a skipper had to be, but he was also kind and caring. His crew loved and respected him. No one ever seemed to use his name, Adam – Adam Benadou. He was just Skipper to everyone.

Because Isaak was seventeen and the youngest, he had to do many of the less exciting chores, like checking the lines and folding the net, bailing water out of the boat when it washed over the side, handling the gaff and baiting the hand lines.

"You can only use a hand line when you're eighteen, Isaak," his father had explained. "That's our rule. Hand lines are very heavy work if there are big fish on the bite."

Frik, who was nineteen, tall and strong, was the next in age to Isaak. He was supposed to help him with the net, as well as with the other chores, when the hand lines were not busy. But Frik was lazy, and anyway he thought himself too big for this. In the mornings, he would turn up late or pretend to be busy with something when he was actually doing nothing at all. He liked fishing with a hand line though – especially to show off in front of Isaak.

The group of Griqua men and their families lived in a cluster of huts tucked away in the forest. The settlement had become known as 'Covie' because of the little cove above which they lived. The people were dependent on the fishermen and what they caught. Where they lived, there wasn't much they could grow to eat. They tried, but the bushbuck, wild pigs and baboons from the forest took most of it. So they ate mainly fish, together with whatever the animals had left. After a good day's fishing though, when there was more than enough for their own needs, they were able to sell some fish. The women and young girls cleaned and wrapped the best and biggest in bunches of wet reeds and took them to the village of Plettenberg Bay. Here, they were able to sell them and buy other food and goods they needed. If there was time after all the selling and buying, they would visit their relatives and friends in the little Griqua community at Kranshoek, just beyond the main village.

On the plateau, high up above the cove, only a narrow dirt road led on to Plettenberg Bay, and to the distant town of Knysna. There was no regular transport along the road, so the women preferred to take the footpath along the shore to the Keurbooms River, where a ferry carried them across to Plettenberg Bay.

The walk there and back was long, and hard. But the women did not think of it as hard. The work had to be done, so they did it cheerfully; singing, talking, or just enjoying the sounds of the sea and the bright flash and chatter of the sunbirds as they swung along the path with the bundles of fish on their heads.

Best of all was all the chatting and exchanging of news with people in the village and at Kranshoek: who was getting married, who had had a baby, who was seeing whom, who was being bad, and who was trying to two-time. This gave everyone enough to laugh and talk about all the way home, so that they hardly noticed how far it was.

For the fishermen, their work was also hard – and could be dangerous. Today, however, the morning was calm and beautiful, and they were looking forward to the day at sea. Together they hauled the boat out of the boat house, down the beach and into the waves. Clambering on board, they first rowed out through the narrow rocky opening to the cove, then hoisted the sail. As it filled with the breeze and the boat gathered speed, the skipper pointed to the south.

"Kyk daar!" he said. "Die vis loop vandag."

Out at sea, a group of sea-birds were swirling around and diving into the waves near the fishermen's favourite fishing ground. This was a sign that all the men understood. The birds knew where the shoals of sardines were, and that was exactly where they would cast their net. Apart from that, they also knew that there was a rocky reef out there, deep below the waves. It had always been a prime place to drop their hand lines. This would be a good day.

The boat moved cleanly in the water. It was a sturdy boat, and although it had been built long ago, the skipper made sure that it was in good shape. He loved that boat, and no one knew better than he how important it was to their community. On its bows he had carefully painted its name: 'Malgas'. He had chosen this name because he always admired the malgas, a sea-bird that was one of the most skilled and successful fishers of the waves.

As the Malgas left the land behind and cut through the slow-rolling swells, the skipper lifted his voice and started to sing. The singing of hymns and psalms was a part of life for the Griquas. But this was *Die Vissers' Lied*, their song, and everyone in the boat knew it.

The skipper sang a line. Then the others answered in a deep, chanting chorus that was repeated over and over, echoing across the hiss of the waves. Through the chant, someone else would lift their voice in another line and, without pausing, the chorus would answer in different words but in the same deep, repeating rhythm. And so it would go on and on. Isaak had a particularly strong, clear voice and he loved singing. So it was often his voice that lifted above the rest, harmonising and blending with the rhythm of the chant, but also soaring clear above it.

The song spoke simply of the winds, the sea, the birds and the fish – but the words were seldom exactly the same. Although there was a pattern that everyone knew, the words could change according to their mood, the weather and the waves. It was a song of asking and of hoping, of happiness and of thanking, and sometimes of fear or of sadness. Any of these feelings could shape the song at any time. Keeping in tune with a mood and its changes bonded them together. They needed this bonding in their boat, on which they sometimes felt so insignificant and alone on that wide, heaving sea.

At last they reached the place where the sea-birds were diving, and furled the sail. Each person knew his job. The net with its floats was cast out over water frothing and jumping with small fish. Then the boat was rowed in a circle as more of the net was fed out from the carefully folded pile in the stern. When the circle was almost closed, they dropped their heavy stone anchor on the reef below. In the meantime, Isaak had baited the hooks on the hand lines. Away from the net, the men let their lines sink down into the emerald green beneath the boat. They all hoped that some big kabeljou or fighting rooisteenbras would be feeding below and would come to their lines – but stompneus, geelbek and many other good fish would also be fine. Some dropped their lines in the deeper water, hoping for a kingklip or two. Called bottom feeders, they were the very best eating fish of all.

First to be drawn in was the net. Those pulling it in said it was heavy. And sure enough, it was bulging with a wriggling, churning mass of silver sardines. These were tipped into a bin in the middle of the boat until it was overflowing with fish. As Isaak was carefully stowing the net again, the skipper leaned back on his hand line and started drawing it in over the gunwales, hand over slow hand.

"Hier's 'n oudtjie," he said quietly. "Kom kleintjie. Kom nou."

Isaak's father always called his fish 'kleintjie', or 'little one'. He said it was bad luck to say it was a 'big one' until it was safely in the boat. But his line was as tight as a bow string and jerked around in the water as the fish fought. This clearly *was* a big one. Slowly but surely, he brought it up. Then Isaak helped him to gaff it and heave it over the side. It was a beautiful kabeljou, fat and gleaming.

At the same moment, Frik called from the other side, "Sjoe! Hier's 'n knewel!" His line was certainly tight as his back bent into the slow haul. "Kom nou, jou skelm!" he swore, as the fish fought back.

At last he dragged it up, and again Isaak gaffed it and drew it over the side of the boat. It was a good fish – but not nearly as big as the skipper's beauty. Still, Frik grinned from ear to ear.

"Hoe lyk *dit* dan, gaffelman!" he laughed. "Now let's have some more bait on this line."

Isaak just glared at him. He knew his time would be coming soon. And he also knew that he wouldn't make such a song and dance over an ordinary fish.

So it went on. The bin was full of sardines, and the skipper soon judged that there were enough big fish in the bottom of the boat.

"Reg, seil op, manne! Time to be moving home." he called.

"Ag, please Skipper. Just a few more," pleaded Frik.

He got a stern look for this.

"Ek't gesê 'seil op' Frik, en dit beteken seil op *nou!* Greed will bring us bad luck – or a boat that sinks because it is too heavy. Laat waai!"

Frik scowled, but he did what he was told. Soon the Malgas was headed for home. The wind had swung round to the south, as it usually did on a fine day. And this was just what they needed. The boat was heavy with fish, but the fresh on-shore wind filled the sail from behind and soon the prow was cutting a white wake straight for the shore.

The skipper struck up a happy line of thanks to the wind, the waves and the fish that had been kind to them that day. The answering chorus came back with an enthusiastic, rolling rhythm, but Isaak noticed that Frik did not join in the chorus.

The people on shore had seen the sail as it was lifted to the wind, pale against the dark green swell of the sea. It was early for the fishermen to be coming back.

"Wat dink julle? Are they moving to a different fishing place?" asked one.

"Dalk is daar moeilikheid!" gasped another.

"Nee. Nee. Kan jy nie sien nie? They're really heading back!" exclaimed a third. "They must have a full catch already. It must be a good one or they wouldn't be coming back so soon."

Which was it? What was the answer?

Excitement rippled through the group of women, children and older men as they watched and waited. At last the Malgas headed into the cove and they could hear the roll and rhythm of *Die Vissers' Lied*. It sounded proud and happy – and then they knew. They knew this had been a really good day.

"Sjoe! Just look at how that boat moves, how deep it sits in the water!" called one of the women. "Kom ons sing vir hulle 'n stukkie."

The women began to clap, sing and dance on the shore. As the Malgas slid into the last small waves, Liesa, a young girl of nearly Isaak's age, couldn't wait any longer. She hitched up her skirts and dashed out into the waves. As the men jumped over the sides of the boat to pull it up onto the beach, she splashed forward.

"Frik! O, Frik! Jy's die beste! What a catch!"

Frik grinned, and was so taken with Liesa's welcome that

the other men had already done the hard work and pulled the heavy boat up onto the beach, before he re-joined them for the fun part; the off-loading of the big fish. The others did not really notice, but Isaak did. He knew Frik's ways too well. He also liked Liesa, and it hurt him to see the way she hero-worshipped Frik.

Isaak and Liesa had been like brother and sister to each other all through their childhood. They'd done everything together. They'd played, they'd swum, they'd laughed and they'd cried; and they'd shared their deepest hopes as well as aches and pains with each other. Only in the last few months had Liesa drawn away. And now it really hurt Isaak to see her with Frik. Frik of all people! He might be tall and strong, but Isaak just did not trust Frik.

He turned away, picked up a fat, wriggling sardine and walked to the dead tree. He looked up at his friend, the fish eagle, and then threw the fish into the waves. "Kuy-yoo kya kya kya," called the eagle and swooped down, lifting the fish with its talons almost as it touched the water. Isaak smiled to see it settle again on the top branch and tear into the fish.

"Net om dankie te sê, ou maat," Isaak said quietly, as he moved back to finish off his chores on the boat.

When the fish had been off-loaded, the big ones spread on a table near the boat house and the sardines in their bin nearby, the women started in with their knives. The fish all had to be gutted and cleaned while they were fresh.

Mara, Liesa's mother, was singing away as she worked. Then she stopped and looked up. "Let's keep one or two big ones for a feast tonight. Daai twee. They look good and fat enough for us all. Wrap the rest in wet reeds. We'll keep them cool here in the shade of the boat house until we go to the village tomorrow morning. They're such beauties, we won't have any trouble selling them."

The sardines also had to be cleaned, split open, salted and then hung up to dry on long lines in the sun. When these droëvis were ready, they were mostly set aside and stored for hard times. But some would be fried up fresh with a delicious garlic and chilli sauce for the feast that night. This was Mara's speciality. She'd learned that she could grow chillies and garlic in her garden: there were few animals that would risk a burning tongue on these!

As the sun sank in a bright orange fireball behind the trees of the forest, Isaak and the other men gathered up a pile of driftwood and lit a blazing fire on the beach. While Liesa and Mara busied themselves with the sardine potjie, whole sides of fish were braaied slowly on the coals, soaking up the smoky flavour and turning golden brown and succulent. People tucked in with relish. There'd not been a feast like this for a long while.

After darkness settled around the glowing ring of coals, there was much contented laughing and story-telling. Then Isaak's father fetched his guitar, struck up a chord, and the singing began. With his father's help, Isaak had made his own blikkitaar. It didn't sound nearly as good as his father's real guitar, but he joined in too, strumming along – at least in the right key and rhythm. The singing went round and round, back and forth across the circle; high voices here, deep voices there, the rhythm and thrum of the guitars always deep in its midst.

Eventually the singing slowly drifted into silence. Tired, but contented, people wandered up the hill to find their beds. But as the moon was still bright Isaak felt the need to be alone for a while. This had been such a good day, yet his heart still had a nagging ache in it; an ache that was only made worse as he noticed Frik and Liesa, hand in hand, strolling off behind the dunes. Isaak walked down the beach and sat facing the sea, letting the quiet hiss of the waves on the sand and the shining, silver light over the sea soak into his being. Then softly, very softly, he began to pluck a gentle tune on his guitar. It was soothing, and he began to feel better for it.

All of a sudden there was a sharp and angry cry from behind the dunes: "Nee, Frik! Nee!"

He turned just in time to see Liesa, sobbing and running across the dunes towards the path up the hill. His immediate feeling was just to get to Liesa; to comfort her. He raced after her. But when he got close, she turned, saw him, and simply ran on.

"Los my uit, Isaak! Just leave me, please!" she called over her shoulder. "This isn't your business. Keep out of it!"

Chapter Two

The Ache in Isaak's Heart

In the days that followed, Isaak tried to forget about what was happening between Liesa and Frik. This was what she'd asked. So, as far as he could, he ignored them and went about his own business. But he missed her. He missed those times when they would just sit together and talk, so easy and close. And he missed being able to drop in to visit at her parents' hut whenever he felt like it. It had always felt like a second home to him, but now this had changed too.

Liesa lived with her father, mother and grandfather. Her father, Gert, was quite a lot older than Mara. A year or so back, he had decided to leave the crew of the Malgas to make way for Frik as the boat really needed strong, young men. Now he spent much of his time fishing off the rocks: something that he was good at, and enjoyed above all else. Like Liesa's grandfather, Oupa Andries, Gert was a warm and kindly man, and she loved them both dearly. When Isaak had come to visit, Oupa Andries always had a story to tell, or Gert would tease him gently with a bright and mischievous twinkle in his eye: things that Isaak now missed as well.

Liesa' mother, Mara, was generous, and always had an open door to anyone; especially to Isaak who had been in and out of that door since he was a baby. But she could also be tough and outspoken. She took no nonsense from anyone. She'd cared for and loved Liesa, but she'd always been firm with her as well. She was a tough and determined woman who worked hard in the community, and she'd brought Liesa up in the same way. Isaak liked her: she was straight, and you always knew where you stood with her. But he was not sure that Frik would find it so easy with Mara!

Frik's mother, on the other hand, was not a tough woman. The man who was Frik's father had disappeared before his child was even born. Frik was really all she had after that, and she'd spoiled him – simply allowing him to have his own way on almost anything. Now, as a young man, it showed.

More and more, Isaak noticed things that he did not like about Frik. One day, for instance, he'd noticed Frik lounging in the sun in front of their hut, while his mother struggled up the hill with a heavy bucket of water. It was only when Isaak went forward to help that Frik came running down, all smiles and apologies to his mother.

When the weather was not right for the Malgas to go out, the other men usually busied themselves with fixing the net, collecting firewood, making repairs to the fence of branches around the huts and gardens, or working in their vegetable patches. On one of these days both Frik and Isaak had gone out to collect firewood. Isaak had been busy for a while when he came through a gap in the trees to find Frik, flat on his back and snoozing in a patch of sun on the forest floor!

Quite often, Isaak would see Frik take up a spade in the garden, dig a few clumps of earth, then lean on the spade and start chatting to whomever was near. He seemed to especially enjoy flirting with some of the married women. Isaak had noticed this when their husbands, and Liesa, were not around. Still, while he didn't think it was right, Isaak couldn't help feeling a little jealous of Frik's charming ways. With his tall handsome body, his ready smile, and his smooth tongue, Isaak saw how charming he could be. And Frik used that charm whenever there was a chance.

Although Isaak tried to ignore Frik and his doings, he could not. He was afraid for Liesa. He tried, once, to talk to her about this.

"Liesa, I know this isn't supposed to be my business. I remember what you said, and I've tried to stay out of it. Maar Liesa, luister tog na my."

Liesa didn't say anything. She turned her face away from him. But at least she didn't walk away. So Isaak gathered up his courage to speak out at last.

"Liesa you've got to hear me. Frik thinks only of himself. I've seen it so often. And he even flirts with the other women when you're not around. I don't trust him, Liesa. I think he's going to hurt you."

Liesa stood for a moment, then she swung on her heel and stalked away without a word. She had already made it clear that he must keep out of her relationship with Frik, and her reaction just made it clearer. So, while he loved and cared for her so much, he now finally knew that he had to bottle it up and just pretend to be getting on with his own life.

But even as Liesa turned her back on Isaak, her mind was going around what he'd said. "What if he's right?" she thought. "But then I don't want him telling me what to do either. And anyway, I like having Frik around. There's no harm in that... or is there?" She thought it might help if she talked to Hanna.

Hanna was a little older than Liesa and a good friend, so she went off to find her. She was down on the beach collecting driftwood for her mother. Liesa joined her and as they walked slowly along the drift line picking up the driest pieces, Liesa told Hanna what had happened with Isaak and how she felt about it. "So, what do you think? Do you think he's right, Hanna?"

Hanna thought a bit. "I don't know," she said finally. "It depends on how serious you are about Frik, I guess. Are you serious about him, Liesa? It looks like it sometimes. And then what about Isaak himself? You've always been close to him. Wat gaan in jou kop aan, Liesa?"

"Well, it's all a bit deurmekaar," smiled Liesa, a little embarrassed. "I like Frik, and he *is* very good looking. But then... I really like Isaak too – I always have – and I could talk with him in a way that I can't ever seem to talk with Frik now. It's just... just... I don't know, like I want some space from Isaak for a bit. And I don't want him to think he owns me."

"Mmm," said Hanna, "tricky!" Then she looked Liesa in the eyes. "I can't tell you what to do, Liesa. Only you can know that. But I *do* think you might have to choose quite soon or things might get even more tricky."

The days and weeks went by. Liesa turned seventeen. She was looking so beautiful now, and poor Isaak's heart was wrenched whenever he saw her. They talked together sometimes – but just as any others might, and not in the way that Isaak really wanted. The invisible line that she had drawn was still there, and he knew that he could not, must not, cross it.

Often at this time, on days when the Malgas couldn't go out and he'd finished his chores, Isaak would take himself off, his blikkitaar hung over his shoulder, and wander up the river and into the forest. Where the river flowed over a wide sandy bar, he waded across. Then, turning up the far bank, he followed a path up to the edge of the deep forest. There was a rocky shelf there, just as the river turned the corner from the steep, forested gully. This was his favourite place to swim.

On one particularly hot day, he walked up to the shelf and thought about a swim, but then he decided he wanted to wander in the forest first. Perhaps he would swim on the way back.

As he entered the forest, he looked around and found the faint game-path that he always followed. Over time, he'd learned its twists and turns through the dense trees and tangled undergrowth. Some trees had particular shapes that showed him the way – a strange knobwood with three thick trunks sprouting from one stump, then an ironwood with an odd elbow in its main branch, and further on, an old stinkwood standing all on its own. He always checked on these markers on his route up to where the old yellowwood giants grew.

From many stories that he'd heard, and from nearly getting lost himself once or twice, Isaak knew how important it was to follow a route that you knew. It was so easy to get lost in a wild forest. The trees were dense, the undergrowth thick and tangled, and if you didn't know where you were going you could walk in wide, repeating circles, getting nowhere, until you dropped with exhaustion.

But Isaak knew what he was doing, and he loved the forest. The leaves underfoot were thick and soft, so treading gently, he walked absolutely silently as though he was floating on a sea of green. The wind sometimes sighed through the topmost branches of the trees, but underneath it was always quiet and calm. Only the occasional, throaty 'krok krok krok' of a lourie, or the whistle of a bulbul, echoed through the silence.

The trees themselves were always a wonder to him. Slowly, with the help of his father who knew the forest well, he'd learned to recognise the different trees: stinkhout and ysterhout, assegai and essenhout, and many more. And then, of course, the giant Outeniqua yellowwoods themselves: the ones that people called 'kalander'. With their massive, tall trunks and great spreading branches hung with moss, these trees had ruled over this forest for centuries. They were truly the ancient guardians of the forest.

Sometimes, he liked to sit at the foot of one of these trees, with the trunk at his back, and just quietly play his kitaar. It felt as though he was in a vast cavern of deep green light, the trees like huge pillars holding a roof up far, far above him.

But today it felt hot and airless under the thick canopy. So Isaak made his way back to the rocky shelf. Despite the quiet of the forest, he still felt restless and his heart remained heavy in his chest. Perhaps a swim would help.

He put his kitaar down and shed his clothes beneath the gnarled and stunted old yellowwood tree that had grown into the rocky shelf itself. The water beneath the shelf was clear, deep and golden-dark. It was a beautiful place to swim. The water felt cool and silky, and Isaak floated on his back, watching the wonderful patterns made by the leaves and knotty branches of the yellowwood against the sky.

As he floated like this, his mind drifted back to a day, a year or so ago, when Liesa and he had come to the rocky shelf together. Throughout their childhood, they had come here to play, to swim, and to talk about anything and everything. But that day had been special.

He was sixteen then, and she fifteen. They were both well aware of one another as girl and boy, but with that easy trust in each other that had grown so deep over the years. The wind had been blustery and threatening on the shore, but the sun was still hot and the rocky shelf warm and protected from the wind. Without a word, first Isaak then Liesa dived in and started to swim up-river. They'd been here so often before, and they knew each other's thoughts so well, that they had no need to speak.

As the river wound its way into the gully, the forest deepened on either side of the dark slice of water. Tall kalanders stood proudly above the other trees, their dark green crowns spreading like great umbrellas over the dense forest below. Smaller kamassie and keurboom trees stood near the shore, the scent of their flowers drifting over the water. Isaak and Liesa swam slowly up the river, the deep quiet of the forest all around them.

Then, as they were wading round a shallow corner of the river, Isaak suddenly stopped dead still.

"Kyk daar," he whispered. "Over there, under the big tree on the far bank."

An otter was having a game with its pups. It hadn't seen them yet, so it came slithering down its mud-slide and splashed into the water. After it came one, two, three pups and plopped into the water. For a while they swam and tumbled around, the pups climbing on their mother, and falling off again, until out she scrambled and came slithering down the mud-slide again – with the pups not far behind. The game went on and on. The otters never seemed to tire of it. Isaak and Liesa were enchanted, watching dead-still in the water. Eventually, with their feet growing numb and thoughts of crabs nibbling at their toes, they quietly turned back. Such a sight was very rare, even up their wild river.

They swam back and sat together quietly on the rocky shelf as the warm air dried their wet clothes. There was no need to talk. It was all there in their shared thoughts and the fresh memory of the otter and its pups. For a long while they sat, soaking up the birdsong and the flash and glitter of the kingfisher as it darted into the water and up again onto its twig.

From up-river they heard the fish eagle call, and then with a sudden rush of its great wings, it swooped down to land on a dry branch on the very top of their yellowwood tree. They both held their breath – it was *so* close. They could see it right above their heads, huge and majestic, with its long curved beak and snowy-white head and chest. Softly, Isaak picked up his kitaar and twanged a high 'kuy-yoo' on the strings. There was a pause, and then an answer from high in the tree: 'Kuy-yoo kya kya kya'. Isaak and Liesa smiled at one another.

Then quietly, so as not to disturb it, Isaak told Liesa all about the fish eagle and the weather: how it perched up in the forest and not at the cove when bad weather was on its way, how it seemed to know long before they did, and how the other fishermen did not believe his story.

Liesa listened closely. Then she looked into his eyes. "I believe you, Isaak," she said simply.

Gently, Isaak took Liesa's hand and felt her palm, warm and soft in his. A glow slowly spread through him. Her eyes were so wide and beautiful as she looked at him. Slowly, ever so slowly, he leant forward and softly kissed her cheek.

"Ek hou van jou, Liesa," he whispered. "Ek hou so baie van jou."

She leant her head on his shoulder. "Ek hou ook van jou, Isaak," she murmured. There was a long pause. "But you know... I've known you for so long – van kleins af. You're like a brother to me, Isaak. That... that's how I feel now." She sighed, her head still on his shoulder.

They sat quietly for a long while, the water lapping gently against the shelf, 'lap... lap... lap... lap'. That sound remained in his mind for a long, long time. There were just so many mixed-up feelings wrapped inside it.

Isaak sighed, and dragged himself out of the water. So much had happened since that day. He missed that closeness he'd always had with Liesa, even if she did feel he was like her brother. And this thing with Frik rankled him – like a deep thorn in his side that he couldn't get out; that he didn't know *how* to get out. He picked himself up, dressed, and made his way slowly back down the river; the ache still pressing heavily on his heart.

Chapter Three

The Song in the Guitar

The months passed by, and slowly the days grew shorter. The winter winds began to blow from the north-west, bringing angry squalls and driving rain with them. There were sometimes calm days in between, when the fishermen could go out and the fishing was often good then. But, as winter drew on, even these days became fewer and fewer. The villagers' huts became cold and damp, and food was scarce. These were hard times. But, even then, they knew how to survive.

They still had the droëvis that had been salted and dried earlier in the year. This was used sparingly. Mostly, the fish was eaten with a thick porridge made of mielie-meal they'd bought when times were good. Usually they had patats as well. These grew in their gardens during the summer, and there was usually enough, after the rooting of the wild pigs and the gnawing of the porcupines, to put some away for the winter. Beyond this, the gardens gave them a little green food, although even this grew poorly in the winter.

When the tide was low, the men, women and children often went out together onto the rocks to collect shellfish. The good swimmers in the group also dived in the channels between the rocks to see what they could find. Isaak and Liesa were amongst the best swimmers. Frik, though, was not – he stayed well out of the water and collected limpets or mussels where the waves couldn't reach him. So these were times that Isaak enjoyed. He could dive together with Liesa, without crossing that invisible line that was still drawn between them.

On a grey and threatening day, when the boat couldn't go out, they all gathered on the rocks. With a deep breath, Isaak and Liesa plunged into the swirling waters of a deep gully and twisted and kicked themselves to the bottom. Liesa searched the rocks and deep crevices for alikreukels and the camouflaged shapes of perlemoen. As fast as possible, she prised them off with a knife and stowed them in her bag. Isaak, meanwhile, was after kreef. They were hard to find, but today he was lucky. He saw a pair of long feelers waving out of a crevice, and with a quick plunge and grab, he pulled a huge spiky kreef out of its hiding place. Then he saw another, but he was running out of air and had to burst through onto the surface. Liesa burst through beside him, and they gasped and spluttered, waving their catches above their heads.

"Wat's als in jou sak... klippe?" teased Isaak when he saw Liesa's bulging bag.

She splashed him in the face.

"Wag net, Isaak!" she laughed, "I'll beat your kreef yet."

Dumping their catch up on the rocks, they raced back and dived in again. Isaak was after the other kreef he'd seen, but Liesa spotted a fat seekat hiding in a dark, rocky crevice. A big, fleshy seekat was perhaps the best find of all, but also the most scary to catch. She hesitated for a second, then advancing slowly she screwed up her eyes and plunged her hand deep into the crevice. The seekat immediately squirted its black ink into her face and wrapped its tentacles round her hand and arm. As fast as she could, she kicked to the surface, turned its head inside out, and threw it on the rocks. Only then did she take a deep breath and really look at it. It was a really big one. She could be proud of that.

When Isaak eventually came up holding two kreef this time, Liesa just stood there, her hands on her hips. "Well," she said, a smile twitching at the corners of her mouth, "only kreef again?"

Isaak clambered out. When he saw the size of the seekat, he had to admit defeat. "Alright Liesa, you win this time!" he said. And they both laughed as they carried their haul over to join the others.

It had been a good moment. But it all came to an end when Liesa rushed over to show Frik her catch...

Isaak stalked off, picked up a stone, and threw it angrily into the sea. "Verbrande Frik!" he muttered to himself. "There's got to be a way through this!" But the answer was not clear – not clear at all.

Apart from the shellfish that others had collected, and Isaak and Liesa's haul, some of the men had also been fishing from the rocks. The trouble was that there were only three proper fishing rods and reels in the whole community. These were expensive things, and few could afford them. Still, the men took turns with the rods as they all enjoyed rock fishing. There was plenty of bait in the gullies, and fish like mosselkraaker, janbruin and galjoen – although mostly smaller than the deep-sea fish – continued to come in. Today, Gert and two others came back with a fair catch. So there was enough food, and, apart from Isaak, people felt cheerful as they made their way back up the hill to the huts.

In the dark, cold evenings of winter, Isaak usually sat with his father at the fire outside their hut. They lived alone, as Isaak's mother had died some years before. He and his father got on well. Mostly, they talked about fishing, or what was going on amongst their people. Often his father brought out his guitar and they sang together. Sometimes it was hymns or psalms they all loved. Other times it was *Die Vissers' Lied*, or one of the endless variations on it.

There were also times when his father played alone: haunting melodies plucked from the strings like drops of musical rain. Isaak always watched closely when he played this way. He wanted so much to be able to pluck the strings like his father. But his own blikkitaar was not made for it. Although he'd learned to pluck some simple tunes on it, the tin guitar was really only meant for strumming.

His father had noticed Isaak's interest and began to teach him. Isaak was delighted. They spent many hours together as he learnt the technique of plucking, and how to bring out the many tones and moods that a real guitar holds secret.

Isaak learned fast. Even when his father wasn't there, he worked on the technique. That winter he practised and practised until, eventually, the guitar felt as though it was part of him. His fingers moved then with lightning speed over the strings, so sure of themselves that he barely had to think about them. They answered to something deeper inside him; his mood, his wishes, and his deepest feelings. Eventually, over those long months, he got to a point where he was unlocking the songs of the guitar with even greater skill than his father. Isaak could make that guitar vibrate with so much passion and excitement that people's feet could not keep still beneath them. His music could lull a man into a dream of gentle winds, sighing waves and the wind-swept call of sea-birds, or pull at a woman's heart-strings and bring a lump to her throat.

One evening in the spring, on the day that Isaak turned eighteen, he and his father were sitting playing the guitar and singing outside the hut. Isaak felt a special bond with his father that evening. He felt a quiet, confident pride in his new status as an eighteen-year-old. Although they'd sat like this through many evenings, that night felt different. He was playing and singing with his father as a man now – not a boy.

At last they fell quiet. Shifting his chair a little, his father turned to face Isaak.

"My seun," he said, "You've a great gift with music. With your voice, you sing as well as anyone I've ever heard." He lifted the guitar and plucked it thoughtfully. "But now I've seen how quickly you've learned to make this guitar sing. And you make it sing with the feelings that are deep inside you. There are few who can do this. It is the great secret of a guitar."

Isaak beamed. His father was a man of few words; words that were always well chosen. And he did not praise often, but when he did, he always meant it. So what he'd just said was like music to Isaak's ears – but a very different and special music.

For a while, they sat in comfortable silence, both simply breathing in the warm evening's quiet, and the far-off chant of the night-jar. The guitar lay resting gently on his father's lap.

"You know, Isaak, this guitar was my father's. He was one who could make it sing too – like you do. I've played it and loved it, but never has it sung for me as it did for your grandfather – and now for you. Dis in die bloed, Isaak, in die bloed."

Again, his father lifted the guitar and drew a gentle, thoughtful tune from the strings. It had felt the stroke of so many hands in its life, this guitar, that its neck and body shone and glowed with wear. His father paused. There was a damp gleam on his cheek, but he smiled, and turned to his son.

"Hier Isaak," he said. "Dis nou joune." And he placed the guitar gently in Isaak's arms. "You're a man now, so use it well, my son. Use it well."

Chapter Four

A Flash of Silver

Earlier in the year, still during the winter months, Frik had started behaving strangely. One morning, when the day was fine and the other fishermen had already gathered at the boat house to launch the Malgas, they noticed that Frik had not yet arrived. He was often late – but never this late.

The skipper was angry. He marched back up the hill to the huts. There, he found Frik sitting hunched up at the back of his hut while his mother anxiously tried to get him to move.

"Kom, Frik!" growled the skipper. "You can't do this. We can't go out with one man short. Jy weet dit mos. Roer jou boude!"

Frik just scowled and hunched up tighter. So the skipper had to lift him by his collar and drag him to his feet. Only slowly then, unwillingly, did he follow the skipper out of the hut and down to the boat.

A while later, he disappeared up the path to the village and didn't come back for three whole days.

Liesa was really concerned. What had got into him? When he returned, she took his hand. "Where have you been? What is it, Frik? Wat gaan aan?" she asked him kindly, but with worry written all over her face.

"Ag, niks! I just don't like it here, Liesa. I wanted to get away, that's all."

"But tell me what's *wrong*, Frik. Is it... are you... are you tired of me?" she finally managed to say. But Frik could not look her in the eyes. He bent down, picked up a stick of firewood, and impatiently threw it into the bushes.

"No, of course not," he said. "Moenie laf wees nie." And with that, he walked away.

After this, however, he started to go away more and more often. He'd dress up smartly and say he was going to the village to buy things. Of course, he never did. But he'd come back days later and collapse in a heap, drunk or exhausted – or both. Isaak suspected what was going on, but he was watching Liesa anxiously to see what she made of all this.

At first, she still believed that Frik really *was* simply needing a break. After all, she wanted to believe this. But gradually, as he came back time after time with nothing to show for his expedition, and no explanation except more and more obvious lies, she began to doubt. The Liesa who everyone knew as so bright and cheerful, became a sad and dull Liesa. She knew now, whatever Frik's lies, that he was spending time with another girl. Whether it was up in the village or elsewhere, she didn't care. She simply knew that she'd been betrayed. Worst of all, she felt shamed in front of all the people she held dear: her mother, father and grandfather; Hanna; and most of all, Isaak.

Frik had now missed several clear days when the Malgas had had to go out a man short. Both the skipper and the other fishermen were really angry with him. The boat needed its full crew and Frik's absence just made things more difficult for everyone; and in winter, dangerous even.

The women, who realised what was going on, were angry too. A little flirting was one thing, but Frik's lies and the cruel way he treated Liesa was not something they were going to accept lightly. Frik had gone too far. In their small community, no one should act like this. He started to feel it from all sides. He was ignored. He was cold-shouldered. He began to realise that he wasn't wanted.

One evening, Isaak was out collecting firewood when he met Frik stumbling down the forest path. Isaak stood up, blocking his way. Frik smirked, but Isaak just glared at him – a smouldering fire in his eyes.

Frik raised his fists, swaying unsteadily. But he wasn't so sure of Isaak now. He had filled out and grown strong in the last while, but more than anything he had a look about him that made Frik see him differently. He was facing a man now, and not a boy – and an angry man at that.

He dropped his wavering fists. "Ag, Isaak. Kom nou. Vat 'n dop, man. We're boat-mates, aren't we?" whined Frik.

Isaak was furious – blind with the anger he'd bottled up for so long.

"Jou slang!" he hissed, and spat on the ground.

The insult stirred Frik. Clumsily, he lunged forward. Isaak side-stepped and thumped him hard in the belly. He'd wanted to do that for a long time, and it was what he deserved.

With a gasp and a whimper, Frik doubled up, clutching his belly. Isaak wanted to hit him again. But then he looked at the pathetic, whining figure in front of him. He wasn't even worth it.

Isaak simply turned his back. "Get out of here! We don't need you, Frik. Skoert!" he growled. And he walked away, leaving Frik lamely clutching his sore belly and his half-empty bottle.

Isaak tried to speak to Liesa – to reassure her that whatever had happened, he still loved her. But she wouldn't listen.

She just covered her face in shame, turned away from him and, without a word, disappeared into her hut. Isaak was hurting too. And he felt frustrated that Liesa wouldn't speak to him. But he didn't know what else he could do. He simply had to wait for her to come out of the dark place she was in.

Liesa was indeed in a dark place. She just couldn't face anyone. Her mother started to get impatient with her: Mara had no time for moping. But Oupa Andries was more understanding. He took Liesa aside.

"Wat makeer, my kleintjie?" he asked gently.

Liesa put her head in her hands and broke down. "I… I've been so stupid, Oupa… so blind and stupid!" she sobbed. "I should have broken off with Frik long ago. Hanna warned me. Even Isaak tried to warn me. I love Isaak, but I was too proud: I didn't want him telling me what to do." She sniffed some more. "Now I'm just too ashamed to even talk to him," she wailed.

"Toe nou, toe nou, my Liesatjie," he said, putting his arm around her shaking shoulders. "It'll come right. You'll get over it. You're a strong girl, I know. You've seen through Frik now – what a skelm he is. And Isaak's still there. The right moment will come, Liesa. It will come."

Liesa looked up into that wise and wrinkled old face, "Dankie, Oupa." She said simply. "Dankie."

At last Frik really did leave. He packed up his things and told his mother that he was going to live in Kranshoek near Plettenberg Bay. She cried and held onto him, but it was no use. He left, saying goodbye to no one else, not even Liesa.

Not long after Frik's departure, a spring day dawned bright and clear, and all the weather signs were right. Isaak was excited. This was to be the first fishing trip since his eighteenth birthday. At last he could join the men on the hand lines. Since Frik was no longer around, the skipper had invited Jantjie, a young boy of fifteen who'd been itching to join the crew, to go out on the Malgas.

"Jantjie, load up the lines!" called the skipper. "Opskud! Opskud!"

Isaak felt a thrill as he heard the new command. He was now one of the men, and Jantjie would take on the chores. Isaak helped him of course. That was the way things worked on his father's boat, and Isaak respected this. But first, before anything, he remembered to glance up at the dead tree. Sure enough, the fish eagle was there, its white chest glowing in the early morning light.

The Malgas headed out as usual, the skipper steering it skilfully between the great shelves of sharp rock on each side of the cove. There was a narrow channel of deep water in the middle that had to be followed carefully. Those rocks could easily smash and sink a boat if they missed the channel. No-one knew this better than the skipper.

They headed out to their favourite fishing ground. There were no sea-birds whirling and diving today, but that didn't bother them. If they found a shoal of sardines on the surface, that was luck. It was the hand lines they relied on, and the fish-rich reef below. All morning they fished beneath a hot, burning sun. They caught some medium-sized fish but, for all their hard work, there was little to get excited about.

Just when the skipper was thinking about calling it a day, Isaak felt a heavy pull on his line. He planted his feet wide, firmed his grip on the line, bent his back, and started slowly, slowly drawing the line in over the gunwale. His heart was beating hard: perhaps this really was his first big

fish. But he didn't say a word. A fish was not caught until it was over the side and safely in the boat, and he didn't want to make a fuss, or spoil his luck, until the fish was right there.

Under his breath, however, he whispered quietly, "Kom. Kom my mooiding. Let's see your silver flash."

The boat was heeling to one side with the weight on the line, so the fishermen moved to the other side and got their lines out of the way. Only Isaak's father stayed close.

"Daar's hy, Isaak. Slow and steady. Slow and steady," he encouraged quietly. "And be ready for the run when it sees the boat."

Isaak's arms ached with the weight and tension on the line. The sun beat down hot on his bent back, but he didn't even feel these things. His whole mind and body were concentrated down there in the deep green water, feeling for the movement of the fish; ready for its sudden swerves and dives as it fought against the heavy drag of the line in his hands.

The sweat was now pouring off his body and his hands felt slippery, but he couldn't pause to wipe them. He strengthened his grip as much as he could and drew hard against the gunwale. Suddenly, there was a flash of silver in the green water below; the fish ran for it. Although it, too, was nearly spent, this was its last great effort to escape the line and the threatening shadow of the boat above it.

The line burned through Isaak's hands. It whipped against his legs, snaking out through his palms and cutting a swerving, deep slice in the water. But he didn't let go. Although the line seared his hands, he was determined, and he was strong. So he braked hard, as hard as he could. The line cut deep into the grooves in the gunwale: grooves that, over the years, had been made with the weight of many lines and many strong fish. But this fish was stronger than most, and it was not going to give up easily. Only slowly, agonizingly slowly, did the pace of the fish slacken. Gradually, hand over hand, he began to draw it in again.

It was really only minutes, but that last, tense haul seemed like hours to him. His father stood ready with the gaff. At last, the now sluggish gleam and twist of the fish could be seen as it hung, exhausted, in the transparent green water below. It was a huge rooisteenbras.

The skipper himself gaffed it and hauled it over the side. With a quick club on the head with his heavy wooden kierie, the fish's thrashing was stilled, and it was out of its misery.

It was such a beauty, and it had fought so bravely. Isaak stood stunned and quivering. So many feelings flooded through him at that moment: the physical pain and ache that he felt in every inch of his body; his pride as his father put an arm over his shoulder and congratulated him; and a sadness too. He could still feel the thrust and surge of that beautiful fish while he'd held it at the end of his line. Although it was a wonderful catch and lay there, broad, long and shining in the bottom of the boat, it was now a dead thing. More than anything, that feeling of vibrating energy that he'd held in his hands was what he could not forget.

Isaak's legs sagged beneath him. He couldn't help it. He sank to the floor of the boat, his head in his hands and his body shaking.

The others saw this as a reaction to the strain. Their bodies recognised it. They also knew what the first really big one felt like. So they were kind to him. They patted him on the back, congratulated him, and helped to coil the line that lay tangled at his feet. Then they baited and dropped their own lines again. Perhaps there were more where that one had come from...

Isaak recovered, but he did not drop his own line. He busied himself helping Jantjie and showing him how to use the gaff as the others brought in a few more good-sized fish. Soon it was time to be moving back. The sail was hoisted and the skipper set the song going. Isaak joined in the chorus, but his voice did not soar that day. His feelings were still too mixed up.

In fact, over the next week or two, Isaak's feelings seemed to be constantly mixed up. He was up in the clouds one minute and down in the dumps the next. Sometimes he felt angry with Liesa for the way she still hung back from him. At other times he sensed she was coming out of her shell a bit and he felt hopeful. He was happy, on the one hand, to be accepted as an adult member of the crew now. On the other hand, he also felt a nagging worry; a restlessness. He couldn't quite understand it. Although he enjoyed the challenge of the catch, he never got used to having to kill the fish he caught. He was unsure of whether fishing was what he wanted to do for the rest of his life. But what other choice was there? Nothing in his life seemed to be clear.

Chapter Five

A Gift Sent From the Sea

Not long after Isaak caught his big rooisteenbras, his cousin, Braam, came to visit from Knysna. He was a bit older than Isaak, but they'd seen each other every now and then over the years and were good friends. Braam also liked singing, so he joined Isaak and his father in the evenings when they sat outside the hut. Braam was impressed with how well Isaak had learned to play the guitar.

"Listen, Isaak," he said one evening. "There's such a need for people who can sing and play like you in my part of the world – for weddings, birthdays and all kinds of celebrations. And in Knysna, you know, they'll pay for it too," he added with a smile. "Why don't you come and stay for a while. We could make up a group."

Isaak looked thoughtful. He really liked the idea. He'd begun dreaming about making something of his singing and his music, but up until now he couldn't see how to do it. He'd also begun thinking – ever since that first big fish – that although he was loyal to his father and the crew of the Malgas, he may not be cut out to be a fisherman. There was perhaps another path for him. Still, he wasn't sure. The boat needed a full crew.

He glanced uncertainly at his father.

Then he turned to Braam. "I'm not sure about the boat,

Braam. I'm not sure that they can do without me now. Frik's left, and Jantjie's still too young."

Isaak's father looked at him. "What did I say about a gift, Isaak?" he said softly. "Don't you worry about the Malgas. We've always solved our problems, and we can solve this one. Maybe you should try out the music idea in Knysna. If it works, you could perhaps help us more than you think. There are different ways to help each other here…"

Isaak beamed. "And I will help, Pa" he said. "You'll see, I will."

Braam was keen to leave as soon as possible. But Isaak wanted a little time. It was not that he had much to pack up – only his few clothes and the guitar. He wanted time to say goodbye. With his boat-mates, the fishermen, this wasn't simply a matter of a word or two and a shake of the hand. It needed plenty of slow talk over cups of hot, sweet tea. This was the way things happened there: no rush, and time to let the thoughts and feelings sink in.

But most of all, Isaak wanted to clear things up with Liesa. He could not leave without telling her what he was doing, and why. And he could not leave without, at least, knowing how the wind blew with her.

He'd noticed, since Frik had left, that Liesa had begun to brighten up a bit. She was now moving around doing her usual chores and spending time with Hanna and her other friends. But somehow that special Liesa spark was still not there. And she continued to hang her head whenever he was near. Isaak couldn't make out why she was avoiding him. He simply didn't understand the depth of shame she was feeling.

As the time drew near when he'd agreed to leave with Braam, Isaak became worried. "How can I do this?" he thought. "How can I break the ice and get Liesa to look at me – and talk to me, really *talk* to me. I just can't leave before this."

Then he had an idea.

Before the time of Frik, when they still did everything together, he and Liesa would sometimes wake very early in the morning. Before the sun was up, they'd make their way across the rocks to the long beach that lay to the east of them. It was a beautiful beach, long, white, and as clean as a sheet in the first light of day. They ran and chased each other along the flat sand, dashing through the shallow backwash of the waves until they fell panting on the dunes. Then slowly, they'd make their way back, this time following the wave line on the sand, hunting for that rare and delicate jewel of the sea: a nautilus shell. These shells were paper-thin – so they had to hunt for them early in the morning before they were damaged by careless feet or pecking birds during the day.

Often they came away empty-handed. Or one of them would spot one on the sand, only to find that its thin shell had already been damaged in the waves. But sometimes, sometimes, they'd find a perfect one: glowing translucent white, with its delicate whorl and pattern of rays spread like fans on either side of its secret inner cavity.

"This has got to be it," thought Isaak. "Perhaps... perhaps, if I can find just one of those shells and bring it to her now, it might help to break the ice between us. I don't know. But I must try."

He set off the very next morning. He hunted. Up and down he hunted; and again, up and down the wave-line. But there was nothing but a broken nautilus shell, and that would not do. There was only one more day to go now before he and Braam had to leave. Isaak went to sleep with a knot in his stomach.

The next morning he was up again before the moon had even set. Isaak was not one to give up easily. He made his way carefully over the rocks in the dim light before dawn and arrived on the beach just as the eastern sky was throwing its pink sheen across the long, flat stretch of wet sand. There was a slight mist over the waves, and the beach seemed to float in a light of its own: as if at the beginning of time. It felt very special that morning. Surely the sea had thrown up a gift for his Liesa this morning, of all mornings.

He did not rush. He scanned the wave-line, then walked slowly along it, head down, gently pushing clumps of seaweed aside. He'd almost reached the end of the beach, and his heart was beginning to lose hope, when he saw the gleam in a patch of seaweed. Gently, he lifted the shreds of purple aside and there it was, whole and perfect – a gift sent from the sea.

It was still early when he found Liesa at the spring, about to collect a bucket of water. He cradled the delicate shell in his hand and walked slowly down towards the spring. He didn't want to surprise or frighten her.

"Môre," he said quietly, but with his heart in his throat.

Liesa ducked her head.

"Môre," she murmured. But at least she did not turn away.

Isaak moved closer. "Liesa... I... I found something for you," he said, almost choking, he was so nervous. "Hierso." And he held out his hand, the shell glowing softly in the cup of his palm.

Liesa looked, and looked. She didn't move, or even glance up at Isaak. She just stared, almost mesmerised, at the shell. Then slowly, as if in a dream, she reached out and traced the nautilus's whorl with the tip of her finger. Slowly Isaak closed his hand around hers and smiled shyly as she looked up questioningly. Then she burst into tears.

"Ai Isaak, Isaak," she sobbed. "Ek's *so* jammer... *so... so...* jammer."

Rather clumsily, Isaak put his arm around her. In a rush, he found himself saying "Liesa, I love you! I always have, and I always will... and nothing that's happened can make any difference to this."

"But I've been such a fool, Isaak. I let that Frik hook me like a fish... and I never saw through him... what a liegbek he was. And I knew you were trying to tell me, but... but I didn't want to hear you. Ag, Isaak! How can you forgive me for this? How can I ever lift my head again?" And she looked searchingly into his eyes.

"Well, you *have* lifted your head, Liesa. You have. See!" he said.

He wanted so much to kiss her at that moment, but there was something that held him back. At last, he knew Liesa *was* back with him; but did she really *love* him. And as more than a brother? It was too soon... and he was not sure, could not be sure.

Liesa had heard, of course, of Isaak's plan to go to Knysna with Braam. Their community was too small for such news not to travel to every ear. But, at least now, he was able to tell her why he wanted to go, and why it was important to him. He told her of his hopes and uncertainties. And he promised to be back for Christmas. Perhaps he would know how things were going with the music by then, and perhaps... perhaps... but not too soon. It was all still only a hope and a dream.

The journey to Knysna was long and hard, up and down across many hills, and along the muddy road that ran through dense sections of forest. It took them two days to get there, but Isaak and Braam had lots to plan and talk about, so the time passed quickly.

As they crested the hill above the town, Isaak gasped. Braam had talked about Knysna and its beautiful lagoon, but Isaak had not imagined how big it was. He'd thought it would be something like the cove that he knew, perhaps a bit bigger. But there it was gleaming in front of him, what seemed like miles and miles of it stretching from the great cliffs at The Heads where the sea washed in, across to the far hills, and right up into the forest.

Then there were the houses: big, grand houses such as he'd never imagined before; and smaller wooden houses clustered together in the valley below, so many of them. After what he'd been used to, he couldn't believe that there were so many people living together.

Feeling excited, and just a little nervous as well, Isaak followed Braam down the hill until they finally reached the wooden house where Braam's family lived. Braam's mother was Isaak's aunt, and she had always had a soft spot for him since her sister had passed away. She was glad to see what a fine young man he'd grown into. She welcomed them in, and put bowls of hot soup in front of them. Then, as the excitement settled, they told her and Braam's father of their plans.

Braam's mother was enthusiastic. "I think it's a wonderful idea," she said. "People around here will welcome a group who can sing and play at weddings and other celebrations."

But Braam's father looked more cautious.

"Yes, it is a good idea," he said slowly. "But think about

this... it's not that I want to knock your idea... it's just that people have to live, you know."

He paused to light his pipe. A silence had fallen round the table, and both Isaak and Braam felt tense. What was coming next? But Braam's father's voice was not unkind as he continued.

"It will take a while for you to get a group going. You'll have to practise and build up quite a few songs. And then people have to hear about you before they'll invite you to play for them – let alone pay for it," he explained.

"In the meantime, you're a strong and healthy young man, Isaak. Braam has a job at the saw mill and he earns his keep. You're very welcome to stay with us, but there are young children in this house who need food, clothes, school fees, books. It's a good idea, Isaak. But we can't carry you – you must understand."

Isaak looked crestfallen. He hadn't for a minute thought that he'd just live off Braam's parents. But, also, he simply hadn't thought of how long it would take before he could bring in some money; or of all the things that were needed here. At the cove it was all so different.

Braam had an idea, though. "They're always short of men at the saw mill," he said. "If you're alright with it, Isaak, I'll introduce you to the foreman and we can see where that goes. We'll always have time in the evenings and at weekends to work up the group – and who knows, we could still fly sooner than Pa thinks."

There was a chuckle round the table at this. At least it broke the tension. Isaak smiled. "That's fine by me, Braam." He turned to Braam's father. "Ek's jammer, Oom. But don't worry, please. I'm not afraid of hard work. I'll make this right."

The next day was Monday, and Isaak went with Braam to the saw mill. The foreman said he could use another pair of hands in the yard. And, there and then, Isaak was set to work, helping Braam and several other men to carry and stack planks. By Friday he had a pay packet in his hands and was able to make a weekly contribution to the household. He felt good about it, and was even able to put some money aside.

Chapter Six

Die Vissers' Lied

Work at the mill was not easy; all-day-long lifting, carrying and stacking planks – and they were heavy planks, broad and long. There was always noise as well: the saws screeching and grinding in the background, people shouting, the rumble and clatter of the huge trailers loaded with logs that were drawn down to the saws. It was tough for Isaak. He didn't mind the work so much as the ugliness of the noise. He really missed the peace of the cove, and the easy, natural sounds of the sea and the forest. He began to wonder why he'd left Covie in the first place.

Also, he learned that the logs were cut mostly from stinkwood and yellowwood trees that were felled in the wild forest behind Knysna. He thought of his own forest. It hurt him to think that trees like these were being cut down in the forests here. But there was little that he could do about the great logs and planks that now lay chopped and sawn in the yard.

"At least the woodcutters haven't found our forest behind the cove – not yet anyway," thought Isaak to himself. "I hate to think what could happen to our place if they did."

Despite all this, Isaak got on well with the men in the yard and enjoyed working with them. They were a cheerful bunch and it was not long before Isaak, with his love of singing, got them going as they worked. There was nothing like the rhythm of a song to work to, and it helped Isaak blank out the noise in the background as he concentrated on the singing. The men really enjoyed it too. Because they lifted and carried together to the rhythm, it made the work feel lighter and less tedious. Most of all, it raised their spirits so that by the end of the day, even if they were tired, they felt better than usual.

Isaak and Braam, in the meantime, had been planning how they should put their group together.

"You must be the lead, Isaak. But we need a few others to join me in the chorus," said Braam. "It would sound a bit lame with me alone," he added with a chuckle.

"I don't know about that. You've got a voice like ten men, Braam!" laughed Isaak. "But seriously, I've been thinking too – and I don't think we need to look too far. With all the singing we've been doing in the yard, I've noticed four of those guys who've got a really great sense of rhythm, and with good voices too."

"Yes, I know exactly who you mean," said Braam. "Dumisani, Pieter, Frans, and that big, strong guy with the deep voice, Senzo. Let's see how they feel about it."

Sure enough, all four were interested and it wasn't long before they'd gathered together for their first practice. Isaak suggested that *Die Visser's Lied* should be their theme song; it was flexible, so they could adapt words to suit just about any occasion. But most of all, it was a song that he loved, and one he could always put his heart into.

It wasn't difficult to teach the others. They all sang well, and caught on quickly to the pattern and rhythm, and how the mood could be shifted and changed according to the lead. Braam, Senzo and Dumisani, who all had deep bass voices, formed the central group behind Isaak, while Pieter and Frans, with lighter tenor voices formed the flanks.

Isaak himself had a voice of remarkable range and strength, so while he sang the solo lead accompanied by the guitar, the bass and tenor voices wove together in rhythmic chanting, to and fro behind him.

The group worked on other songs and arrangements as well. Some were hymns and psalms that people knew well. These would be important for weddings or funerals. They also developed a range of songs for different occasions: rhythmic, working songs like they sang in the yard; songs with a beat that would set people's feet dancing; or quieter, harmonising songs that were just good to listen to. Ideas came from different members of the group and, if the idea seemed good, they worked on it together until they'd refined it: words, sequences and rhythms that were different, but still carried the special balance and sound of the group.

On his own, Isaak worked on solo pieces on the guitar: some from his time at the cove; some that were new and echoed his feelings while living and working in Knysna; and some that spoke wordlessly of his love and longing for Liesa.

But it wasn't easy. And it all took much more time than they thought.

Since there wasn't much room in Braam's house, and the younger children had to do their homework, they couldn't practise there after work. It was also difficult at weekends when Braam's parents wanted to relax or have friends round. It was much the same where the others lived.

They tried practising at the back of the yard after the day's siren at the saw mill had sounded. But the atmosphere was wrong. It was so dreary there with the planks stacked around them, and all the associations with their daily work.

The whole smell and feel of the place hung around them like a big cloud.

Isaak, Braam and Senzo were still very committed. They really wanted this group to work, but Dumisani, Pieter and Frans were gradually losing heart. They tried and tried and made some progress, but it wasn't right. They all knew it.

The group stood in a huddle in the grey cold of the evening, their shoulders slumped. They couldn't go on like this. There seemed to be no way out.

"What are we going to do?" asked Isaak desperately. "We can't just give up! There's got to be a way to make it work."

"Ag, ek weet glad nie," said Frans. "There's nowhere else to go – and I don't like this place. I'm tired anyway after work, and just being here makes me feel more tired."

"Ja, ek ook," added Pieter.

Dumisani just looked glum.

"Listen," said Braam. "You guys sing so well, it would just be too bad if you gave up. We've got a real chance if you can hang in with the group."

There was silence. Frans, Pieter and Dumisani were not going to budge.

Isaak stood deep in thought.

"OK, here's an idea," he said at last. "It will take us longer to get ready, but it might be the only answer. Let's give up the practice after work. We can stick to weekends. And I've got a thought about where we could do it." Isaak turned to Braam. "You know that big tree on the hill behind your house? We'll feel better up there than in this dump – and it would also be shady when it's hot. We won't be disturbing people. And if it rains, we can just call it off for the day."

Frans and the others looked a little brighter. "Dit klink 'n bietjie beter vir my," said Frans. Pieter agreed. Dumisani was still not so sure. But... "OK, I'll give it a try," he said finally.

"Good," smiled Braam. "I think it's a great idea, Isaak. And I like it up on the hill. I used to play there as a kid and there's a good feeling up there. So let's go for it – this Saturday then, under the tree!"

Isaak and Braam were right. Their mood really did lift up on the hill. The group drew together and they sang with enthusiasm, and now as a tight unit. It wasn't long before a whole series of songs that had just not sounded right at the yard began to gel together and take on a final shape.

Although they hadn't intended it, their decision also had another positive spin-off. In no time at all, the sound of their singing had drawn a crowd of youngsters playing on the hill. As word spread from them to their parents and others, the crowd grew. People applauded and asked for more. Sure enough, they were soon invited to sing at a wedding. Perhaps Braam would be right after all. Perhaps they were going to fly – even if only a little sooner than his father had predicted!

Word soon got around in the community about how good the group was. Invitations, not only to weddings but to all kinds of events, came in thick and fast. They were now booked up for a string of weekends ahead. One day, when they were performing at a particularly large function, Isaak was approached by an elderly, well-dressed man.

"I've heard much talk about you and your group, Isaak. And now I've heard your playing and singing myself. I think you're good," said the man. "Let me introduce myself. My name's Le Fleur."

They shook hands, and Meneer le Fleur continued. "I own the Fisherman's Tavern – you may know of it, Isaak. It's the one down near the docks, where the fishermen bring in their boats."

Isaak nodded and smiled. He and his friends had often

been there for a chat and a bite to eat after work. It was a friendly place, and people liked to go there: it wasn't one of those smart, expensive places in town where only a few people could go.

"Well," said Meneer le Fleur, "I've been thinking about putting on some entertainment on Friday and Saturday evenings. Would you and your group be interested? I'll pay you a flat rate for each evening, and you're likely to pick up some tips on top of that."

Isaak was excited. This was a great chance. "Dankie, Oom! Baie, baie dankie!" he said. "But I must speak to the group first. I think they'll like the idea though."

The group members met to discuss the idea. They all agreed that it was a good chance, not only to earn more, but for the group itself to move forward.

But there were some practical problems.

"It's not going to be easy on Saturdays," said Braam. "We have all those bookings for the afternoons – and then we'll have the evenings too. What do you think? Can we do it – and still do it well?"

"There's getting home late at night, too," added Senzo. "I think I can sort out any skollies who come my way! But we live in different parts – will you guys be alright?"

After some discussion, they agreed that the afternoons and evenings would not be a problem. They would just have to make sure that afternoon bookings in the future were not too late, so they could at least have a break between performances.

The problem that Senzo had raised, however, was a real one. Despite his size and strength, even he could be vulnerable to a gang of skollies late at night: and there *were* gangs around, particularly near the docks. They knew it.

Isaak said he'd speak to Meneer le Fleur to see if there was some solution. He understood the problem immediately; he knew the area only too well himself. Gangs had broken into his tavern several times.

"I think I can help," he said. "I have a small truck I use for getting supplies – you could all fit in the back of that. It'll mean that you'll have to wait until I close up, but then I could drop you off at a point closer to all your homes."

Everyone in the group was pleased. They were due to start the next Friday, so during that week they even met after work at the saw mill to practise and refine their pieces. They were so buoyed up by this chance to prove themselves that they didn't even notice the place and how tired they were! By Friday, they were set to go.

Their first evening was a great success. People had heard that the group was to be performing at The Tavern, as it was affectionately called, so there was a good crowd. The opening *Visser's Lied* went down particularly well. There were several fishermen there who knew the song – even if it differed a bit from place to place – and they soon caught on to the chorus and joined in. In fact, all the songs that had a good, rousing rhythm went down well, with people singing, clapping and dancing to the music.

What was amazing was what happened in the quieter pieces; especially when Isaak played solo on the guitar. As he plucked his first few bars, the noise in The Tavern sank away slowly until you could hear a pin drop. People were entranced with the silver drops of sound that he drew from the strings, and the lilt and sway of the moods he created with such feeling and skill. When he finished such a piece there was always a pause of absolute silence… then a roar of appreciation and applause.

Le Fleur was delighted. This was going to be very good

for his tavern. He paid them a generous flat rate – more than they'd expected – and a number of people handed tips to Isaak.

At the end of the evening, Isaak called the group together. He put all the tips and the flat rate together, and then shared it out equally into six piles.

"But Isaak," objected Braam, "You can't do that. You're the leader. You must get more."

"Sure," said Pieter. "What could we do without you? We'd be nothing." And the others nodded their heads at this.

Isaak just laughed and shook his head. "Well, what should we do then – also give Braam more because he thought of the idea; or give Senzo more because he's got the deepest voice? Come now, we all need each other here. That's the way our group works; the only way it *can* work!"

So the matter was settled, and the group bonded: their loyalty to each other, and to Isaak, was like that between the skipper and his crew. This was what Isaak knew and respected. It would always be this way with him.

Starting off, the group found Fridays and Saturdays quite tough going. On Fridays, they had to work all day in the yard, perform in the evening, and then wait until closing time before getting home – exhausted. Saturdays were not as bad, but two performances, one after the other, were also tiring. Still, they got used to it soon enough. And anyway, they were carried along by their success.

What with the Saturday events, and working at The Tavern, almost everyone in the community got to know about them. People loved their music. It felt like their very own and they took the group to their hearts. They were proud of this group of young men from their own ranks who were doing so well. It gave people a sense of hope. It could be done.

More than anything, though, the youngsters were becoming inspired. They joined church choirs to learn to sing. Some even tried starting their own groups. Whenever they could, Isaak and the other members of the group helped them out, giving advice and encouragement. One of Braam's younger brothers became really keen on learning to play the guitar. He watched Isaak whenever he practised, and Isaak showed him some chords and the simple strumming technique that he himself had started with. Quietly, when he was not looking, Isaak started to put together a blikkitaar for him. Christmas was a while away yet, but if he could get it finished, there would be nothing like this as a present to encourage the youngster. Isaak knew from his own experience.

Chapter Seven

Lied van die Bos

Work at the saw mill continued. Although the members of the group were earning well from their performances, this was only on weekends. They needed to work during the week as well. The weekly wage allowed them to cover their living costs so that what they earned from their performances was extra. Most used the extra money to help their families. For Isaak, the small community at the cove was his 'family', so he saved as much as he could, and thought of Christmas when he'd promised to visit them all: his father and Liesa above all.

Apart from this, the members of the group would have felt different from their families and the people around them if they did not go to work in the mornings. And none of them wanted this. Their group, their songs, and how they felt about themselves, were all part of the community. This was what people loved about them. The group themselves felt good about it. So going to work in the week, like everyone else, was important.

The weeks went by. Christmas was no more than a month away now. Isaak had already made his plans, and the group had agreed that, for two weeks over Christmas and early New Year, they would all take a break. The yard would be closed over that time, and although Le Fleur was disappointed that they wouldn't be around over the busy festive season, he understood that they needed a break.

Whenever he had the time, which was not often, Isaak busied himself finding presents for all the people who were special to him at the cove. He also had to think about what supplies he could manage. His pile grew bigger and bigger, and he started worrying about getting it all there. Braam, of course, said he'd come to help but it was still a lot, even for the two of them. Then Senzo stepped in.

"Don't you worry. I'll carry this whole lot on my back, and not notice the difference," chuckled Senzo in that deep voice of his. "And anyway, I want to meet this girl that Isaak's so mad about. I want to make sure she's good enough for him!"

Isaak laughed, and gave Senzo a punch for good measure. But he came away wringing his hand. That man was made of iron!

"Thank you both," said Isaak. "It'll be great to have you along anyway. And just you watch out, Senzo. Liesa's so beautiful, I don't want you running off with her. I'll have to beat you up if you do."

They all fell about laughing at the thought of this. And Isaak was thinking how lucky he was: to have friends like this; and to have had such amazing success with their group. If only things could come together with Liesa. That was all. He longed for her *so* much.

The next week, Isaak had a surprise. The foreman in the yard had heard that he had grown up with a wild forest all around him, and he wanted him to go out with the forest team. In all the noise of the saw mill, Isaak had so missed the forest and its quietness. And working there would be a welcome change from the yard with its lifting, carrying and stacking all day.

"The forest foreman needs a good 'tree spotter' to go ahead of the cutting and felling team, Isaak. Your job would be to mark the trees for felling – straight, well-grown ones, especially stinkwood and yellowwood. Could you do that, Isaak, without marking the wrong ones or missing any good ones?"

"I could," said Isaak. "I know the trees well."

"Good, you can start tomorrow," said the foreman. "And, if you can prove yourself, your pay packet will rise too."

Isaak was pleased on one hand for a change from the routine in the yard, and a chance to get into a wild forest again. But on the other hand, he was sorry his friends wouldn't be with him. They all enjoyed working together in the yard, even if the work was hard and boring.

"Still, there'll always be stories to tell them after work, I'm sure," he thought. "The forest's never dull, that I know."

But Isaak's first day in the forest was not what he thought it would be.

As they approached the part of the forest where trees were being felled, it looked just as though a tornado had ripped through it. Giant kalanders, some as ancient as those he knew at home, lay crashed to the ground, their great branches twisted and shattered like huge broken arms and legs. Others trees lay across them. And, with their weight and size, all these felled giants had crashed through the forest around them, smashing the younger or smaller trees into twisted spikes, stumps and heaps of broken branches.

Somehow, Isaak had not expected to see what lay in front of him. In the yard, he had known that the logs that came in, and the planks that were sawn from them, had all been beautiful trees in a forest like his own. But seeing sawn up logs and planks was not the same thing as seeing these dead and broken giants lying on the smashed-up forest floor.

Isaak felt he wanted to turn his back on it all. "Am I to be part of this now! How will I face Liesa, Pa, and the others at home?" Then, with horror, he thought, "What if the woodcutters were to come and do this to our own forest!"

Slowly, unwillingly, he went forward to get his instructions. He had no option now. But at the back of his mind a simple plan was forming. If he could not stop the destruction, he could perhaps make a small difference… and he'd certainly try.

The foreman showed him the next section that was due to be cut. It was a large area, the trees still tall and untouched, stretching from the woodcutter's track, down a sloping hill to a stream at the bottom. His job was to search out the right trees, and the best ones, cut and clear the brush around them, and then mark them clearly with a thick band of white paint.

The woodcutters in the other section were already at work. The sounds of the saws were already rasping the silence of the forest. More ominous still was the regular chop, chop, chop of the axes as men cut, rhythmically but inexorably, into the trunk of another ancient giant.

Isaak made his way into the new section. He could still hear the saws and axes in the background. But some of the stillness of the forest lingered on here – despite the constant reminder of what was coming to it. He trod quietly through the soft, leafy undergrowth, following a line down the hill and stopping when he had to clear and mark a chosen tree.

It always hurt him to do this, especially when it was a kalander. It was as though he was personally condemning it to death.

As he got closer to the bottom of the hill and the stream, the forest became much denser. Trees were closer together and the undergrowth grew thick around them. It was more difficult to find and single out those trees that the woodcutters wanted. Isaak cleared and marked a stinkwood that stood out a little more obviously. Then he burrowed through the vines, bushes and creepers that surrounded a particularly dense patch. His sharp eyes had spotted something in there that he hoped no one else would notice. Sure enough, well hidden by the surrounding growth, stood a sturdy young yellowwood; not a grandfather, but certainly straight and well grown enough to be taken by the woodcutters. He smiled and patted the smooth, round bole of its trunk.

"You, I will not mark," he murmured quietly to the tree. "Grow strong, tree. And shed your seeds around. Perhaps you can father a few new yellowwoods around here at least."

This was the first part of Isaak's plan. As he made his way slowly through the section, clearing and marking those trees that could not be missed, he was always on the look-out for others that were well hidden. Compared to the number of trees that he had to mark, there were not many that he could 'save'. He could not be too obvious about this or his whole plan would fail: the trees would be found, and then cut down anyway. So he was careful. But, by the end of the day, he knew that there were quite a few well-grown stinkwoods and yellowwoods in this part of the section alone that had a chance of living on. With luck, and if he was not found out, there would be more on the days to follow. As he left the section that afternoon, Isaak felt a little better than he had in the morning.

When he rejoined his friends that evening, he told them of what he had seen; of the devastation in the forest that lay behind the logs and planks in the yard. And he told them about his job, and how he hoped he had saved at least a few trees for the forest.

"But what if they find out, Isaak?" asked Frans. "You'll lose the job, and you won't get any raise."

"Ag, ek gee nie om nie," said Isaak impatiently. "You don't know what that forest looked like. I've tried to tell you, but you'd have to see it yourself to know. It was really terrible. I just couldn't live with myself if I hadn't done something. Can you see that?"

Frans nodded, but he still seemed unsure. The others, even Braam, also looked unsure, and a bit uncomfortable. Isaak was really going on about this. But trees were trees, and people used them for wood, so what was the big problem?

Isaak realised that he would not convince his friends. You had to have lived in a wild, unspoiled forest to know it and love it as he did. Liesa would understand, he knew, and perhaps other people at the cove. But this was where he was different from his friends. So he accepted it, and kept his feelings about the forest to himself after this.

However, there was one thing he did do, and that was to compose a solo piece on his guitar. The second part of his plan had actually been to create a song with the group: a song that spoke of the forest and its wounds. But then he thought better of it. Such a song would not work if the other members of the group didn't feel as he did. So he composed a guitar piece instead. He called it simply *Lied van die Bos*.

Through natural runs and chords that he drew from the guitar, he subtly suggested the sigh of the wind in the tree-tops, the hush of soft rain, the call of birds, and the dance of sunlight through the leaves. He let his feelings for the forest – those deep feelings that he'd grown up with – speak through his hands. The sound of the guitar was gentle, liquid, evoking feelings of timelessness, of peace and tranquillity.

But then suddenly, harshly, the song came to an abrupt end. Harsh, ugly sounds of chopping were hammered out on the body of the guitar. An agonized screech and tearing sound was drawn from the strings, and then there was a final, discordant crash of chords.

When he played it for the first time at the tavern, people were entranced by the first part, and then shattered, disturbed, by the ending. They came up to him and asked why the piece had ended like that.

"In our own forests, this is what is true," was all he said.

Chapter Eight

A Fishing Rod and a Dress

At last the time for the Christmas break drew near. All the members of the group were tired. The past few weeks had been hectic. They'd not only put on extra performances because of all the community events that happened at that time of year, but Isaak, Braam and Senzo also had to make their final preparations for going away.

Isaak had finished the blikkitaar and put it safely away in a cupboard. He wanted to give this to Braam's brother along with his presents to the family, on the day he left. His other presents, to be taken to the cove, were wrapped in bundles that he, Braam and Senzo would carry.

There was one thing, however, that he could not wrap. It was a gleaming cane fishing rod, together with a large wooden reel, that he'd bought for his father. The skipper had always wanted a rod like this for the times when they had to fish off the rocks, but he'd never bought one for himself. He always spent his money on things needed for the Malgas, because he knew that the boat was the lifeline of the community. This was typical of his father's generosity and care for others, so Isaak was especially pleased about being able to give him something for himself at last.

For Liesa, he was not so sure. He wanted to give her something special, and yet he wasn't certain that this would be the right thing to do. In his mind, he debated backwards and forwards: "What if she still doesn't really love me? What if she feels I'm pushing her too far?" But in the end, he listened to his feelings: "I *want* to give her something special. I love her, and it just feels right. So it must be right."

He had no problem knowing what she needed – and wanted. But finding it was another thing. He knew that she had few dresses, and those that she did have had been mended a hundred times. Liesa cared for her clothes. They were always clean and you had to look carefully to see where they'd been mended. But the fact was, those few dresses were really wearing out.

So Isaak looked for a new dress that would please her. The smart shops in town were a little strange and daunting. Still, he took a deep breath, lifted his head, and walked in as if he had been doing it all his life.

He looked up and down the racks of dresses. There were so many fancy styles, colours and shapes to choose from that he felt really confused. None looked right for Liesa. But then a dress in a simple style caught his eye. It was the clear, green colour of the sea as it washed over the sand in their cove. He knew this was the one. She'd look so beautiful in it. He asked the shop assistant if he could buy it.

She looked at him kindly. She could see that he had *not* been doing this all his life!

"Are you sure that it is the right size?" she asked.

Isaak's jaw dropped. He simply hadn't thought about that. He had no idea what Liesa's dress size was.

"I... I... don't know," he said, a little panic in his voice.

"Now, don't you worry," she said. "Perhaps we can work this out. Is she about my size, do you think?"

Isaak looked at the young shop assistant. It was true, Liesa *was* about her size, perhaps a little taller. He nodded.

"Alright, wait here a moment," she said, and disappeared into the back of the shop. When she came out, Isaak was stunned. He couldn't help staring. She was wearing the dress, and it looked absolutely beautiful on her; a fraction too long, but that would be fine for Liesa's height.

"That's wonderful! Just right, and... it looks beautiful, just beautiful" he said, admiringly. "Thank you."

The young girl could not help blushing a little at Isaak's enthusiasm, and his admiring look at her. After all, he was a very good-looking young man. But she ducked her head modestly, turned quickly and disappeared again into the back of the shop. She came out with the dress, and wrapped it in pretty paper for him.

"If it still isn't right, bring it back. If she can't come in herself, I'll be very happy to try on another one for you," she said with a glowing smile.

Isaak went away, very happy with the present he'd found for Liesa. But a small part of him couldn't help but remember how beautiful the girl had looked, her modest blush, and her glowing smile. It had been such a long time now since he'd seen Liesa. He was tempted, over the next few days, to find some excuse to go back into the shop – just to see the shop assistant. But then he stopped himself.

"Am I just another Frik?" he asked himself. "No, of course not. I know I'm not! And I know it's Liesa I love – Liesa only." He sighed. "It's just been so long. I need to see her so much now – so, *so* much."

The last few days really dragged past. They seemed to take forever. Finally, it was time to go. At supper time, the evening before they were due to leave, Isaak gave out presents to all of Braam's family. Everyone was pleased, and Braam's mother and father both said how happy they'd been for him to stay with them, and that he must come back. Braam's younger brother was over the moon with his blikkitaar. He couldn't stop playing it all through the evening, until Braam himself had to quieten him down.

"Môre's nog 'n dag, boet," he said kindly. "And if you practise hard, you never know, you could be another Isaak on the guitar!"

The next morning, they set off at dawn. True to his word, Senzo carried a huge bundle, with Isaak's guitar stowed safely amongst the other parcels. Even so, both Braam and Isaak carried fair loads themselves, with the fishing rod also over Isaak's shoulder.

It took them two whole days again, and they had to find shelter under some thick bushes and trees for the night. They were used to doing this if they had to, but it was always a little frightening. There were elephants in the forests around Knysna – those few that had not been shot by the ivory hunters. Any snap of a branch at night made them start and hold their breath. But they had chosen a place on the outer edge of the forest where it was fairly safe. The worst they experienced was the hum and sting of hungry mosquitoes!

The next day was also long, and their heavy loads made the going tough. Only as the sun was sinking behind the mountains did they finally enter the forest path that led down to the huts above the cove.

Isaak was keen to make the fishing rod a surprise for his father, but he wasn't sure how to hide it – it was so long! As they tramped down the hill, the forest growing dark around them, Braam had a thought.

"Why don't we hide it in the trees just near the huts? You could surprise your father with it tomorrow morning," he suggested. So they did just that.

The candles and fires of the little community were now in sight, and they almost ran the last few steps. Dropping their heavy bundles outside, they burst in on Isaak's father. He almost fell over with surprise and delight, and tears were in his eyes as he welcomed Isaak home and shook hands warmly with Braam and Senzo.

In no time at all, others had gathered around the hut. And what a welcoming there was, with hand shakes, claps on the back, and everyone talking at once.

Isaak couldn't contain himself. He looked around for Liesa. At last he saw her. There she was, standing back a little, her eyes shining as she looked at him. Over all the heads, their eyes met for a long, long moment. His heart turned over inside him – and he knew. At last he knew. Quickly, he made his way to her through the small crowd. They held each other tightly, Liesa smiling from ear to ear with sheer happiness.

"Oh, Isaak, Isaak, it's been *so* long!" she sighed, nuzzling into his neck.

"Hai, wat gaan daar aan!" called someone.

"Not in public, you two!" shouted someone else.

"Too long, my Liesa, too, *too* long!" murmured Isaak, leaving her reluctantly as the teasing around them grew.

Mara had got a quick soup together, smelling deliciously of fish and her invariable wilde knoffel sauce. Others had made fresh vetkoek cooked on the coals. They brought it all to the skipper's hut where the three young men were fed and spoilt with happy attention. Everyone wanted to know how it had gone with Isaak in the big town.

"It's been good," he said. "Braam and his parents have been really kind to me, and I've made some good friends, like Senzo here."

"But the music, Isaak? What happened with your plans to make music?" called out one of the fishermen.

"Let *me* tell you," said Braam. "I know Isaak. He'll just say 'it's gone fine' or something like that. In fact, Isaak has become famous in Knysna. He got five of us to join him in a group, Senzo and me included. We sing with him. He leads us, and he plays that guitar – the one the skipper here gave him. He plays with such skill that he can make people dance and laugh and cry just as he wants. We perform at weddings and all sorts of community events, as well as at the Fisherman's Tavern, in town. That's where we have a regular show every Friday and Saturday night. I tell you, your Isaak has become a star."

People clapped and shouted when they heard what Braam had to say. But Isaak shook his head, and held up his hands.

"It's not true! It's not true!" he said when things quietened down. "Braam has made it sound as though it's all me, and it's not. He's right about what we do. But none of it could have happened without all six of us in the group. It's what we do together that people like. And anyway, it wasn't my idea in the first place, it was his!"

Isaak turned to Braam and Senzo. He put his arms over their shoulders. "I wish it could be all of us standing here; Dumisani, Frans and Pieter too," he said. "But I'm very proud to be standing here with you two, at this moment, in front of all my family and friends."

At this, there was a great cheer from every person around them. And the three young men were almost swamped with the warmth and congratulations showered on them. People wanted to hear more, but Isaak, Braam and Senzo were clearly exhausted, not only with the long journey, but also with all the emotion and feelings of the evening. Isaak's father stepped in.

"Môre is Kersdag," he said. "Let's give these young men a chance to rest. Tomorrow there'll be all the time in the world for us to talk and hear more."

So people drifted off to their own huts. Isaak gave Liesa a last quick kiss, and then he and his two friends collapsed on a mat in the skipper's hut – and didn't know a thing until the birds woke them early the next morning.

First thing, after wishing his father a happy Christmas, Isaak asked, "Pa, would you mind giving me a hand to get some firewood. We're going to need it tonight." So off they went together up the path through the forest. When they came near enough to where the fishing rod had been hidden, Isaak started breaking off dead branches and suggested that his father try a little further up. Suddenly there was a cry of wonder.

"Kyk hier, Isaak! What's this – a brand new fishing rod just standing in the trees!" exclaimed his father.

He turned to look at Isaak and was met with a broad grin. "Happy Christmas again, Pa!" laughed Isaak.

At first, his father could not believe it. He held the rod in his hands as if it would break apart and vanish any minute. Then slowly, with his one hand, he stroked the shining wood of the reel and up the cane of the rod. He looked up at Isaak, his eyes sparkling.

"Dankie, Isaak! Dankie, my seun! This means so much to me." And he hugged Isaak to him with one arm, while the other held the precious rod.

"And Isaak," he added as he stood back and looked at him, "You've used your gift well, my son – really well. And for that, above all else, I am very proud of you!"

They returned to the huts, and while his father was testing the rod, whipping it in the air and feeling its balance and power, Isaak took himself off to find Liesa, something hidden in a cloth under his arm.

She was hanging up some washing. "Happy Christmas,

Liesa," Isaak called. "What's with the washing on Christmas morning!" he teased.

"Ag, I just wanted a clean dress for tonight," she said. "Daar's hy, kant en klaar." She smiled. "Happy Christmas, Isaak. You look as though you had a good sleep last night. But what's that under your arm?"

"Well," said Isaak, with a sparkle in his eye, "Close your eyes and hold out your hands."

Liesa took a deep breath, and did what she was told. Isaak took the pretty parcel out of the cloth and placed it in her hands. She giggled. "Right, you can look now," he said.

"En....wat is *dit*? It's such pretty paper, Isaak. I don't want to tear it." But she did. She couldn't wait to see what was inside. Then she gave a squeal of sheer delight as the soft, green material unfolded in her hands. "O, Isaak! Isaak! Dis *wonderlik*!"

Isaak's face was glowing with happiness at her delight. "Put it on Liesa, won't you."

"Nie nou nie, Isaak. I want to put it on this evening – for the Christmas celebration," said Lisa. "That'll be special."

"Nee, nee. I don't mean wear it all day," explained Isaak. "I just want to see you in it now. Then you can change again."

She ducked into the hut and, in a minute or two, she came shyly to the door. The dress looked absolutely stunning on her, and it fitted her perfectly. Isaak couldn't wait. He lifted her in his arms and danced round and round.

Liesa was half laughing, half crying. "O, Isaak, dis my eerste, my heel eerste nuwe rok. Dankie, dankie, dankie!" Then she straightened the dress and looked at him seriously. "But how did you know to get one that fits me so well?"

"Ag, well," said Isaak. "That's got to be my secret!" And he laughed and kissed his beautiful Liesa with a long and happy kiss.

Chapter Nine

Harmonies over the Cove

The rest of that Christmas day was spent with much talk and excitement. Apart from some basic supplies like mielie-meal, flour, tea and sugar that he had brought for hard times, Isaak had brought presents of one sort or another for everyone at the cove. Each present had been given thought, and had special meaning for the person concerned. So, for Mara he'd found some spices and curry powders that he knew she would like to use in her cooking, but on which she could never bring herself to spend her limited money. For Gert, Liesa's father, he'd got some hooks, swivels and sinkers: things that were frequently lost with rock fishing. For Jantjie, he'd found a new, shiny pocket knife that he could use for wood carvings, instead of that old broken stump of a kitchen knife. And so it went, something for everybody. There was not a single person who was not delighted with what Isaak had brought.

Braam and Senzo came round with him. Although Braam already knew many of the people, he wanted to greet them and exchange news, while Senzo wanted to meet the people about whom Isaak talked so much. There were many cups of sweet tea drunk that day. Gradually, details and stories about the group came out, and people felt more satisfied. They got a real feeling of how the group had made its mark in Knysna, and how it had not been easy.

In turn, Isaak heard how things had been going on the Malgas and with the fishing. He hadn't heard much of this from his father, who'd gone off to the rocks with his new rod; he just couldn't wait to try it out. But from the other fishermen, Isaak heard that old Gert had had to re-join the crew. He was no longer as strong as the younger men, but despite this, the skipper and the crew were evidently happy with him on their team. They all got on well together, and this was what they felt to be most important. Isaak was relieved to hear that they were all happy about the arrangement. But he still had a nagging concern that perhaps he should be there. He was still young and strong, and the Malgas should not be carrying an older man, especially old Gert who should have been enjoying his 'retirement', with his fishing rod on the rocks.

Isaak heard that the fishing had not been too good. This wasn't unusual, Isaak knew. There were always ups and downs. But there had been several weeks now when the weather was wrong, or the catches had been poor, even when they had managed to get out. It was clearly time for a good day: the community needed it.

Nevertheless, that evening was their Christmas celebration, and even if stock was low, everything was pulled out to make a feast. As the sun sank towards the western hills, people started moving down to the beach.

Isaak, Braam and Senzo were gathering driftwood for the fire when Isaak spotted his father walking back from the rocks at the far end of the cove. He walked across to join him, and to hear about how things had gone with the new rod. As he got near, Isaak was greeted with a huge grin. His father held up a brace of fat fish, held together with a strip of fishing line.

"Nou, toe nou," exclaimed Isaak. "Net betyds vir die visbraai, nè Pa."

His father was excited. "Man, Isaak, you don't know how good this rod is. It's got a cast like I've never seen before – right out into the deep water, no trouble." He laughed and clapped Isaak on the back. "I'll beat Gert any time with this. If he reckons he's the champion caster, wait till he sees this one!" and he chuckled again.

Soon all the people of the little community were gathered together in a circle around the fire. Being Christmas evening, there would be a prayer from Oupa Andries, the oldest man in the group and a pastor in his time, and of course one from the skipper. Then they'd all sing a hymn before the celebratory feast. But Isaak looked around and he couldn't see Liesa. Where was she? She'd be late for the prayers!

Then, just as the last rays of the sun slanted across the beach, Liesa emerged from the forested path. The flaming rays of the sinking sun lit up the clear soft green of her new dress against her golden skin. She seemed to shimmer and glow in the twilight. Isaak gasped. To him, she seemed like a vision, an angel, as she drifted so beautifully towards the group.

People cheered and clapped as she came shyly forward. Comments and teases came from all sides.

"Ag, Liesa, jy's n prentjie in daai rok!"

"Hey, you're a lucky one!"

"Where'd you get it?"

"Gert, jy moet nou hierdie mooi dogter van jou goed dophou!"

Isaak couldn't contain himself. He ran forward and took her hands in his. "You look *so* beautiful, Liesa, *so* lovely!" he said, his eyes shining. Liesa smiled and glanced down demurely. "Dankie, Isaak." Then, lifting her face, her dark brown eyes glowing, she said again, "Dankie, my Isaak."

Poor Isaak, his insides seemed to melt. But he caught himself, and before he did anything rash, he took her hand

and said, "Kom, my eie Liesa," and led her into the circle around the fire.

Oupa Andries stepped forward and the gathering quietened. "Laat ons bid," he said, and with simplicity and feeling he led them through the Lord's Prayer. Then the skipper glanced around at the faces of his people.
"Laat ons dank betuig," he said quietly. His prayer was short but heartfelt. It expressed gratitude for the year past, for the friendship and belonging that they all felt, and for the food they had before them. "Die Here sy dank," he ended.
"Amen!" echoed round the cove. Then raising his voice, the skipper led them into one of their most beloved hymns. The forest and cove resounded with their voices. Then, as the echoes died away, people settled closer to the fire and the cooking and preparation began.

It was a wonderful evening for everyone. The fresh, braaied fish were really good with the other food that had been put together. It gave people hope. With the skipper's luck today, perhaps the luck on the Malgas would change as well. And so the feast was not only plentiful, but people were in high spirits too.
There was much laughing and teasing between Gert, the skipper and the other fishermen. Isaak and Liesa were dancing round the fire, kicking up sprays of sand and chasing each other around. Braam and Senzo had gone for a night splash in the waves, and the others – especially the young women – hung onto each other laughing and cheering as these two hunks of men splashed around in the moonlight like two kids. Hanna led the cheering, her face alight with the fun. She'd taken a bit of a shine to big, good-hearted Senzo, and she couldn't help showing it.

Eventually, things calmed down and people settled round the glowing coals. There were calls of, "Musiek, Isaak! Maak vir ons musiek." So Isaak fetched his guitar. He gathered Braam and Senzo round him, and he said, "Right, what's it to be? Shall we start with *Die Vissers' Lied* in honour of Pa's rod and fish?"

They broke into the song, and even though they were three short, they sounded good with Isaak's clear voice and the depth and strength of Braam and Senzo's voices in the chorus. But this song was too close to the hearts of the fishermen there: they were not going to be left out. Soon the group had swelled to ten strong voices, weaving and chanting to the beloved rhythm of their song. As it came to an end, people clapped and shouted, calling for "Nog! Nog!"

And so the singing went on, late into the night. There were songs that only the men sang; deep, resonating chants that rolled around the cove. There were songs where only the women's voices soared; high, clear rhythms that rippled and hung over the water. And there were songs where all the voices joined together; strong, rousing songs when the sound echoed off the cliffs and high into the air. Liesa, sitting next to Isaak, often joined in with him, their two young voices weaving together in a duet of clear, strong harmonies that rose and swelled high above the rest.

Isaak also played some solo guitar pieces, bringing dancing and laughter with some, and sighs and tears with others. *Lied van die Bos* brought a stunned response as always. So Isaak laid the guitar aside and told his people of what he had seen in the forests behind Knysna, and of how he feared for their own forest.

"Play it again Isaak, won't you," Liesa asked quietly. "We can hear it with different ears this time."

So he did. And people were very moved. Even Braam and

Senzo, when they saw what the trees and the forest meant to the people here, began to understand Isaak's passion.

People were getting sleepy then, so the group – just the three of them – sang a gentle song to end the evening. Their voices rose and sank, threading together in a subtle harmony that felt like soft, textured cloth. When the song drew to a close, a contented silence fell over the group circled around the dying embers of the fire. No one wanted to move. The stars shone scattered above them, and the waves lapped quietly on the shore. It felt so good to be together there, all the feelings of the evening washing peacefully over them.

Eventually, some began to yawn and stretch. People gradually got to their feet, wished each other good night, and drifted up the hill in pairs and groups. Isaak and Liesa walked slowly together.

"You play so well now, Isaak," she said, leaning her head against him as they walked. "En jou *Lied van die Bos* is kragtig. I wonder what those town people think of it."

"I don't know," said Isaak. "I don't know if they understand. Maar wie weet, Liesa? Wie weet…"

Chapter Ten

A Dream and a Water Dance

The day after Christmas was always a holiday for the people at the cove. Other holidays mostly went unnoticed. They worked when they had to, and relaxed when the weather prevented it. But this morning, even though the weather was good, people rose late after the festivities the night before and drifted around their morning chores. Isaak's father had to come and shake the three young men awake, they were in such a deep sleep.

"Kom nou, luisakke!" he called. "It's a beautiful day – and the fish are waiting for us down there off the rocks."

Naturally, he again wanted to spend the day with his new rod. But he wanted a bit of competition and fun too. So off he went in search of Gert to see if he could tease him into taking him on.

Isaak awoke feeling groggy and disturbed. He'd had a really strange dream in the night which he didn't understand, nor could he escape the strange feeling it had created. It kept on going round and round in his head. He splashed water on his face and, feeling a little better, went off to find Liesa. She was the only one to whom he felt he could talk about the dream.

He found her down at the spring again.

"Môre," she called as she saw him coming. Then as he

got closer, "But Isaak, you look sort of pale. Are you feeling alright this morning?"

"Well... not really, Liesa. I had this dream... and it keeps on coming back to me. It was an awful dream. I don't understand it, but it just felt so... so sort of mixed up and frightening. I just can't shake this bad feeling, Liesa."

"Kom Isaak," she said gently. "Come and talk about it." And she led him to a quiet place under the trees.

"You know how it is with dreams, Liesa. I can't remember all of it, or how it started... but the part that sticks in my mind was the Malgas... it was caught in a storm, and waves were crashing all over it. And my father's voice, calling and calling to me on the wind. And the fish eagle too, calling and calling from up in the forest. I was trying to call it back to the cove. I had the feeling that things would be alright if only it would come back... but it wouldn't come. It just kept calling – and me calling – and my father too, calling and calling. Oh, Liesa, it was so horrible... and I felt so helpless, stuck in the middle of it all."

Isaak sunk his head into his hands. He was shaking all over.

Liesa put her arms round him and just held him. Eventually she said, very quietly, "Dis vreeslik, Isaak. What a horrible, horrible dream – so frightening."

Isaak lifted his head and looked at her. "But do you think it *means* anything, Liesa?" he asked anxiously. "Do you think it's a warning or something?"

"Ek weet nie, Isaak. Ek weet nie." Liesa sighed. She thought a while. Then she looked up at him. "But you know," she said uncertainly, "sometimes if I'm worrying, it comes out as something else in my dreams. But I know it's the worry that's coming out, it just *feels* like something else." She paused. "Does that happen to you, Isaak? Is there something worrying you?"

Isaak thought about this. "It's true, Liesa. I do know what you mean. And I *have* been worrying – ever since I heard that your old pa has had to re-join the crew. Even though they all say it's working fine, I'm not so sure. My feeling is that the boat really needs young men – especially as my own pa is not so young himself any more." He sighed. "The trouble is, I know that I should be here, Liesa. The Malgas needs me. But I love the music too... and I'm caught in the middle. It... it really *does* feel like the dream."

Isaak paused, and looked down for a while, thinking. Then he looked up, his face clearer. "I think you're right, Liesa. The dream probably was about this worry of mine. And I must clear it up. I'll speak to Pa. It's the only thing to do." At last he smiled. "Thank you, Liesa. I feel a lot better now."

But Liesa still looked serious. "I don't know if I'm right, Isaak. There might be some other meaning in the dream – I can't tell." Then she smiled. "But if you feel that it's helped, that's good."

Isaak got up and stretched. "Well, it's a beautiful day. Let's not waste it. Our two pa's are going to have some competition and a bit of fun on the rocks. Why don't we go diving and collect some bait for them. Would you like that?"

So Isaak and Liesa, as well as Braam and Senzo whom they'd invited along to see the competition, started to make their way down to the rocks. As they passed Hanna's hut Liesa called out, "Kom saam, Hanna! There's going to be some fun down on the rocks." Hanna didn't need a second invitation with Senzo there!

The skipper and Gert were already hard at it. They were using sinkers only on the end of their lines, trying to beat each other at casting. One would lean back and then cast his line as far out into the deep water as he could manage.

Then the other would do the same.

"Mine went further!" the skipper would exclaim.

"Nooit! Dit was myne!" Gert would retort.

The younger group chuckled as they watched them, arguing away, with neither one prepared to give in to the other.

Isaak came up to them. "What about Braam, Senzo and Hanna being judges for you," he suggested. "Liesa and I will go off and dive for some red-bait in the meantime. Then, when the casting's been decided, you could try a fishing competition."

Gert and the skipper were of similar age, and they'd been good friends for many years. There was nothing that they loved more than to compete with one another on this or that: and then have a good laugh about it all afterwards. Up until then Gert had definitely been the best at casting. He used his own rod, while the skipper had to borrow one of the other two rods. And those rods were old and battered; not good enough to beat Gert with, anyway. But now things were a little different. With his new rod, the skipper really could take him on!

So it was agreed. "We'll decide the casting out of the best of ten casts each," said Braam. "Come, Senzo, Hanna, we'll sit high up on those rocks so we can have a good view of where the sinkers splash into the sea."

"But what if we can't agree?" asked Hanna.

"Well, then we'll have to take those casts as a tie," said Braam.

Gert went first. He found a place on the very edge of the rocks, where the waves splashed around his feet. Pausing for a second with his rod at the ready, he cast high and far out into the dark, deep water. It was a good cast. The skipper chose to stand further back on a flatter piece of rock. With a lightning quick sweep and flick of the rod, he also cast far out into the deep water. Both the competitors immediately claimed that their cast went the furthest. But the judges shook their heads. "First one's a tie," said Braam. "Too close to tell the difference."

So the competition went on. These two were both good, and they were running neck on neck. There had been five ties, and Gert and the skipper had each had two clear wins. Now it was the decider. The tension was running high. Even the judges were sitting excitedly on the edge of their rock.

Again, Gert went first. He bent his back and with a sweep of his rod, he sent the sinker sailing into the sky. But he'd actually heaved too hard, and cast too high, and the sinker curved down from its high point and splashed into the sea – not as far out as he'd hoped. The skipper went next. He steadied himself on the rocks to get good balance, then with a backward twist and a clean whip of his new rod he sent the sinker shooting out like an arrow over the sea. There was no argument this time. The judges were agreed.

"Skipper wen," called Braam, "Not by much, it's true, maar tog die wenner!"

After Isaak and Liesa had left the fishermen they went off to find a good gully to dive in, as well as collect bait for the fishing competition. They wandered quite far over the rocks before they found one where the water was deep and green, not churned up into white foam like the other gullies they'd passed. They took their time. Sitting on the rocks on the edge of the gully, they watched the swells moving gently in and out, sweeping the coloured fronds of seaweed back and forth. The sun was bright, the sky a great arc of blue over the sea, and they were totally alone. There was not a soul in sight.

Isaak turned to Liesa, and took her hand. "Liesa, the last time we dived and swam together, there was a line between us that I felt I couldn't cross; it felt like a thick wall to me then. Do you know what I mean?"

Liesa nodded. She knew exactly what he meant. And, with a twinkle in her eyes, she said, "Kom, Isaak. Swem nou saam met my – and then all lines or walls that were there can be wiped away for ever." And with that, she dived, sleek and clean, into the water.

Isaak was bowled over; not only by the sheer beauty of his Liesa as she'd stood there before him, but also by her daring. Yet it was more than daring, he knew. It was her trust in him, and her love, that had led her to this point. Laughing happily, he plunged in to join her.

They circled, dived and floated together in the gently rocking motion of the swells and the clear, green depths of the gully. They chased each other, then rolled over and over, their bodies softly touching then separating in a gentle water dance that felt quite timeless. When they finally pulled themselves up on the rocks, laughing and hand in hand, it was with something of a shock that they realised how far the sun had moved.

"Liesa, we still haven't got any bait for the fishing competition!" exclaimed Isaak. "Kom, gou-gou!"

Grabbing up their knives and bags, they dived back in again. Fortunately, they were so skilled at this that it wasn't long before both of them had bags bulging with the rubbery-soft cups that held the red-bait in their centre. Hurriedly they dressed again and ran back across the rocks.

The skipper greeted them. "Nou ja?" he said with a tease in his voice. "I never knew you two to take so long to collect a bit of red-bait! Here I've been sitting, waiting to beat Gert at fishing too – and there's no bait!"

Even though they couldn't help looking a little embarrassed, Isaak and Liesa quickly emptied their bags. While Liesa climbed up to join Hanna, Braam and Senzo on the high rocks, Isaak took out his knife to open up the cups of red-bait.

The skipper and Gert baited up their hooks and went off to see what they could catch. "Biggest fish wins," shouted Isaak after them. "I'm going to join the others. See you later."

The sun was very hot now, so the three friends and Liesa and Hanna wandered back to the beach to find a patch of shade under the cliffs. Isaak and Liesa chuckled as they heard about the casting competition; how close it had been, and how the arguments and teasing had gone this way and that between the two competitors. They whiled away the afternoon, and eventually the skipper and Gert appeared over the rocks.

"En toe?" asked Isaak. But he got no answer. "Come on, let's see," he said as they got closer. Rather shamefaced, the skipper showed a miserable little fish, and Gert produced something not much bigger. There was a disbelieving pause, then everyone, including the fishermen, burst into laughter.

"I guess that makes Gert the winner," gasped Braam, still holding his sides. And they all fell about laughing again.

"Vergeet daarvan. Nie met 'n kriewel soos dit nie!" said Gert, putting his arm around the skipper's shoulder. "I'll just have to show you the next time, won't I, Skipper!"

They started walking slowly across the beach towards the path up the hill. Isaak was at the back with his father. "Pa, there's something that's still worrying me. I know Gert's your friend, and that you're happy with him on the crew again. But isn't it better to have a younger man? Shouldn't I be there – for the boat, and everyone's, sake?"

Isaak's father walked slowly on, but said nothing for a while. Then he stopped and looked directly at Isaak, his sharp eyes gleaming amidst their creases. "Do you not remember, my son, what I said before? 'There are different ways to help each other here.' You *have* helped, Isaak. Already, you've done much for us – much more than if you had been on the Malgas. Now, I want you to forget this, please. It's kind of you to think about it, but it's not even a question for me, or for the others." He put his arm over Isaak's shoulder. "What's important is for you to continue to follow the way your gift leads you. Follow it, Isaak, always follow it."

Chapter Eleven
The Dark Cloud

The next morning when Isaak woke, his father had already been down to the shore to check the sky, the wind and the waves. He could hear him calling to Jantjie, and gathering the crew together. Isaak hurried. He wanted to help, at least in the launching of the Malgas. And he wanted to check the fish eagle.

The boat was already out of the boat house, and they were about to haul it down the beach. He ran to join the men in this heavy part of their task. It was only when the Malgas was in the water that he had a chance to look around. The weather certainly looked good. The wind blew gently off-shore, and the swells rolled slow and straight into the mouth of the cove. But when he turned around to look for the fish eagle on its dead tree, it was not there. He could hear it calling far up in the forest.

Isaak was scared. He turned to his father and the other fishermen who were already climbing into the boat.

"Look, the fish eagle's not in its tree. It's up in the forest. It knows when bad weather's coming. Ek beloof julle," he called out. "Please, please don't go out today!"

But the crew would not take him seriously. "Kom nou, Isaak! You've got a thing about that fish eagle of yours. The weather's fine, just look at it," they said. "You can even ask old Gert here – he's seen more than any of us."

Gert looked at the waves and the wind direction, and then he stared long at the sky. "Well," he said at last. "There are just a few wispy clouds moving from the north-west very high up, but I don't think they're moving fast enough. I think it'll be alright. Still, it might be a good idea to keep a watchful eye out today. I don't know about fish eagles, but I do know that weather can come in fast sometimes. Wat dink jy, skipper?"

"Ek stem saam," said the skipper. "We'll watch those clouds. But we need to get out. It's been too long since we had any catch at all. Come, let's get on with it."

All morning the day stayed bright. Isaak began to think he'd been silly. He told himself to stop worrying, and got on with other things. But at midday, he couldn't help himself. He went down to check the fish eagle again. Perhaps it had just been late in coming down to the cove that morning.

When he looked up at the dead tree, however, it was still not there. And he was sure that there were more icy streaks of cloud, sweeping faster now across the high sky.

Meanwhile, on the boat, the fishermen were having a good morning. The fish were on the bite and they were all busy drawing up one good fish after another. They were so busy in fact, that no one remembered to check the high clouds. It was only at about two o'clock that the skipper saw the line of dark clouds, low on the horizon. They were black, threatening, and moving fast.

He didn't wait. He knew what that meant. In a very short time the wind ahead of those clouds would hit them. They had to run for home now, and just hope they could make it before the storm hit.

"Lyne op, en span die seil! Gou-gou!" he called. "There's a storm coming! Roer julle!"

The Dark Cloud

There was a scramble in the boat. The crew knew what to do to set the sail, but they couldn't do this before the last fishing lines had been drawn up. Gert was struggling with a heavy fish that was fighting hard and he couldn't get it up.

"Cut the line, Gert! Cut! We must move!" shouted the skipper, just as the first gust of wind skidded across the water, flattening the tops of the waves.

They set the sail and started for home, but the boat was heavy with fish and moved sluggishly through the waves. "Throw the fish overboard, Jantjie," called the skipper. "It's a pity to lose them, but we *must* move faster."

Soon, dark clouds began to sweep over the sun. In no time it was gone altogether, and the whole sky became dark and threatening.

The wind was blowing harder now. The boat heeled over, and the crew all had to move to the windward side to try to right it. Two men had to hang onto the sail sheet to prevent the wind whipping the sail away altogether. And Jantjie was bailing as hard as he could to get rid of the water that kept on washing in.

"Hou vas, manne! Keep going, Jantjie!" encouraged the skipper as he, himself, fought the wrench and pull of the tiller.

It was no easy job to keep the Malgas headed for shore against a cross-wind like this. But they were getting there. Every now and then, as they crested a wave, the skipper could just make out the grey shapes of the rocks on the shore in the darkness. They were getting closer, but it wasn't easy to see the narrow gap that led into the cove. He strained to see through the gloom, but the brief moments on the crest of a wave were too short for him to be sure.

The wind got stronger and stronger. The sheer force of it now whipped the waves into heaving, swirling mountains around them. The boat climbed up one wave only to plunge done the other side, smashing its bows into the next wave and having to struggle up that one. Water was pouring into the boat. Gert and two others were now all trying to help Jantjie with bailing, but they couldn't keep pace with the water that kept washing over the bows. The Malgas was getting heavier and less responsive to the tiller. Then, on top of it all, a bitter cold rain started lashing down. The men's hands were now freezing as they struggled to bail and to hold onto sail and tiller.

Suddenly a mighty squall of wind smashed into the boat. With a loud crack, the mast snapped. It fell to the side of the boat, tangled in its own rigging, and dragging the sail in the water with it. Without any sail, and with the drag in the water, it became impossible to steer the boat.

"Cut the mast loose! Kap hom weg!" shouted the skipper above the howl of the wind. "We *must* try to row."

They tried, two men to each long, heavy oar, fighting against the wind and the waves that ripped viciously at the oars. But they could barely make headway. More water kept pouring into the boat, making it heavier and heavier. Jantjie and old Gert alone were hardly keeping pace with bailing it out. Wave after thundering wave carried the Malgas sideways. The oars felt powerless against their cruel force.

When Isaak had seen the high clouds at midday, and that the fish eagle was still not there, he was afraid. But he didn't want to spread panic amongst the others. Things would probably be alright. The fishermen would see what was happening with the high clouds, and would turn around in time. The skipper had said they would keep a close watch.

He did decide to go and look for Liesa, however. He needed to talk to someone about his fears. She was at her hut. Isaak called her aside, and told her about the fish eagle: he told her how he'd tried to persuade them not to go out that morning, and about the high clouds and how there were more now, and moving faster.

They both looked up. It was hard to believe that anything was wrong. The sun was still out and it was calm on the ground with hardly a breath of wind. But, sure enough, high in the sky, thin streaks of cloud were now clearly racing across from the north-west.

"Ek's bang, Liesa, *so* bang," whispered Isaak. "That dream... the fish eagle..."

Liesa held him. She could feel the tension and fear in him. "Ek weet, Isaak. Ek weet," she said, trying to calm him. "Come, I think we should go down and look for the sail."

They made their way down the path to the shore. There was no sign of the sail yet. The air was still calm, but the swells were no longer rolling straight into the cove. They were no longer gentle either, and were now moving sideways and breaking in great sprays of foam on the rocks: those same rocks where they'd all been so happily together the day before. Then, high up in the forest behind them, they heard the high, echoing call of the fish eagle. Isaak held on to Liesa's hand. An eerie fear gripped both of them. But they waited and watched: they could do nothing else.

It was some time later that Isaak saw the first ominous black cloud on the horizon. It was still a thin line, but it was growing fast, he could see. Still there was no sign of the sail.

"I'm going to call Braam and Senzo," he said. "There's going to be trouble, I'm sure now. That storm is coming in fast and... and, I don't know how... but there may be something we can do."

He raced up the hill. His two friends were sitting quietly outside the skipper's hut. "Come. Come with me. Quick!" he said, urgently but quietly. He didn't want to alarm other people yet.

Braam and Senzo followed him down the hill, and as they went, he told them what was happening. "What do you think we can do?" asked Braam.

"Ek's nog nie seker nie," answered Isaak. "We can only watch and see what's happening – and then help, when and if we can. But we must be there; they may need us."

By the time they reached Liesa they could, at last, see the sail: pale against the gathering darkness behind. Soon the wind hit them as well. Gusting across the cove, it whipped the waves into a foam, stinging their eyes with salt and sand from the beach.

As soon as the wind picked up and the dark cloud began to cover the sun, the women, children and older people at the huts realised that there was danger. They also came down the hill and gathered on the shore, waiting and hoping; praying that the Malgas and their men would make it through to the cove in time.

When they could see it, the boat appeared to be getting closer, but the waves around it were now huge. They seemed to swallow it completely for minutes on end. But when they saw it again, briefly, it seemed to be too far across: not headed for the entrance to the cove at all. Then the sky became darker and darker, and soon they lost even those brief sightings of the boat behind sheet after sheet of stinging, driving rain.

"Come. We must get to the rocks," shouted Isaak against the roar of the wind. "If they make it we'll see them. But if not... if not... Kom! Maak gou!"

Liesa joined the other people, now clutching each other; staring silently with fear and dread into the driving rain.

Isaak, Braam and Senzo fought their way across to the rocks on the east of the cove. Monstrous waves now crashed relentlessly against the sharp, black barrier in front of them. Salt water and rain drenched and blinded them as they clung to the rocks against the force of the wind. Step by slow step, they moved closer to the teeth of the barrier.

Then sickeningly, dreadfully, but clearly above the roar of the wind and waves, they heard a terrible crash, and then a fearful tearing and splintering.

The sound came from further to their left. Numbly, full of dread, even knowing it, but not yet able to accept the horror of it, the three clawed their way across the rocks. Then splinters of the Malgas began to appear in the foam and wash of the waves. Grimly, they knew what they had to do now. The chance of anyone having survived that cruel smash against the rocks, let alone the mountainous waves, was slim. But they had to try.

"Over here!" bellowed Isaak against the wind. "Gou maak! There might be someone we can help."

It was a terrifying task. As they clawed their way around the rocks, they were smashed and drenched by wave after wave. Seething water sucked and dragged at their legs. Driving, stinging spray soaked and near-blinded them. But battered and frozen, the very terror of it kept them from feeling the dread at what they might find.

Suddenly, Isaak glimpsed an arm moving weakly in the water. As one huge wave retreated, and before the next one came in, he dived in. Fighting the drag of the water, he pulled the limp body up onto the rocks. It was Jantjie, bloody and battered, but still alive. Quickly, he turned him over and squeezed his chest to get rid of the water in his lungs. Then picking him up bodily, he carried him higher up the rocks so that he was out of reach of the waves. Jantjie coughed, spluttered and then vomited the water from his stomach. At last, he took a heaving, stuttering breath, and opened his eyes.

"Ag, Jantjie, Jantjie," moaned Isaak, cradling him in his arms. "Jy's hier! Jy's nou veilig!" Jantjie took a deeper breath, and smiled weakly.

The other two carried on searching. Braam found one of the crew wedged between two sharp rocks, but he had drowned. Senzo dragged a body clear of the waves. It was old Gert. But his head was badly battered, and he had drowned too. In fact, by this time, the chances of finding anyone still alive in the fierce and relentless suck and drag of the waves, had become just about nil.

Bravely, they searched on a little longer, but Braam and Senzo knew now that it was hopeless. Isaak could not tear himself away. He still hoped against all hope. Eventually, Braam had to shout that they should really get Jantjie back. He was shivering uncontrollably. So Isaak picked him up and slowly started making his way across the rocks, as far out of reach of the waves as he could. The other two tried to carry and drag the bodies as well, but it was too difficult over those rocks, and they were heavier than Jantjie. They laid the bodies carefully under some overhanging bushes, and then joined Isaak to help him get Jantjie over the more difficult parts.

When they eventually staggered onto the far end of the beach, the little group of women cried out: high, thin cries shredded by the wind. They ran forward, anguish and horror in their cries and on their faces. When they saw Jantjie in Isaak's arms, they knew, finally, what they had feared the most. The boat had gone, and the rest of their men with it.

But there was Jantjie, still alive. And there were the three young men. They'd been gone so long that the others had been afraid that they, too, had been lost on the rocks. Jantjie's mother ran up to Isaak. Crying out with relief, she took her son from him. It was her turn to take over. She was going to make sure he was made as warm and as comfortable as possible. Jantjie was just able to smile at her.

Chapter Twelve

The Skipper's Tiller

That night a great and terrible sense of shock hung over the little community. Everybody had lost a husband, a father, a son or a friend. Each and every person was stunned; numbed by the sheer horror of the shipwreck. Some sat alone, their eyes just staring into the darkness. Others sat together, holding each other; some sobbing, some simply with heads bowed, silent tears running down their faces. It had all been so sudden, so terrifying, and so totally devastating.

But somewhere, somehow, through the depth of that shock and grief, there were those who were also able to feel for the young men who had made their way onto those savage rocks to try to save whoever they could. Although their loss hung heavy on them, the people also knew that Jantjie lived and breathed, and was now safely in his mother's care. Without Isaak, Braam and Senzo, this could not have been.

After being wrapped in blankets, fed hot soup, and warmed at a fire, the three friends collapsed, exhausted, into a deep sleep. By morning, though still cut, bruised and aching, they knew what they had to do. The storm had blown over in the night, and a weak sun was out again. Bodies would have been washed up on the shore by now, and they could not be left open to the sun and the scavenging eyes of birds and animals. It had to be done as soon as possible; not least because the tide was now low.

Finding the bodies was a gruesome task. It was especially so for Isaak, whose father would be among the bodies, and who knew and loved each of the other men of the Malgas's crew. He was very grateful to Braam and Senzo, who ended up taking on the major load.

Shortly after they reached the site of the wreck, it was Isaak himself who found his father's body. The skipper had been washed up onto some pebbles at the end of a gully. He lay face up, a broken piece of the tiller still in his hand. It was as though, even in death, he was still trying to steer the Malgas and his men to safety. It was too much for Isaak. He broke down and wept and wept, rocking back and forth, cradling his father's head in his lap. The others let him be: he needed this time to himself.

Braam and Senzo eventually found, one by one, the remaining three bodies. All had been badly battered on the rocks, but they were still recognisable. People would at least be able to mourn their loved ones. Slowly, helping one another over the rocks, they carried the bodies one at a time, including the two that had been found the day before, to a level place near the boat house. Here they laid them out, side by side, on the ground under a grove of trees. People were gathered under the trees, shocked into silence as the grim row grew before their eyes. But, as each body was carried in, one or more ran forward, sobbing and weeping, to hold their own for the last time.

Eventually, Braam and Senzo had to disturb Isaak where he still sat holding his father at the end of the gully. He understood. Taking his father's shoulders himself, he and Braam carried the skipper back and laid him next to his crew and his friends. Many sobbed and wept at this moment. Everyone had loved and respected their skipper, and his passing was like a wound to them all.

Senzo, Braam and Isaak dug the grave in the sand under the boat house itself. It felt like the right place to lay the men to rest: their boat, their Malgas, had lain there for so long. They dug the grave long and deep. There was no possibility of making coffins, so Mara organised the women to cut swathes of reeds to cover the floor of the grave, and they had blankets ready to put over the bodies before they were covered. One by one, the men were laid out, lying next to one another, the skipper last. Isaak bent down and placed the broken tiller back in his hand.

Oupa Andries slowly came forward and, with great dignity mixed with pain, he spoke the moving words of the funeral prayer over the open grave.

Then, as the skipper's son, all faces turned to Isaak to say the final words of farewell. At first, he was overcome; he wasn't sure that he could do it.

One by one, his eyes rested on each of those around him. They were his people, his family: Liesa, her eyes on him with such trust, such belief in him; his friends, Braam and Senzo, who had done so much to help; Jantjie, pale and bruised, but miraculously still with them; and the men in the grave, his friends the fishermen, with whom he had worked so long. Finally his eyes turned to his father, their skipper, his skipper.

Isaak took a deep breath. He knew now that he could do it; that he must do it. "Mense," he said quietly. "I must do this in the only way I know how." He asked Braam and Senzo to join him, and then Jantjie too. Liesa had anticipated this, so she'd fetched his guitar from the huts and now silently brought it to him.

Quietly, gently, with head bowed, Isaak began to pluck

the strings of the guitar. Then raising his head, he lifted his voice in the opening line of *Die Vissers' Lied*. The chorus of Braam, Senzo and Jantjie responded, the low rhythmic chant drifting across the little cluster of people around the grave. At first, the song spoke not of grief or regret, but of the wind and the waves, the birds and the fish: as it always had done. Then, as it came to its conclusion, it finally spoke of loss, of love and of the deep sadness that ached in every heart – and the chorus swelled, through its weeping, with the voices all around.

When the song ended, silence fell over the group and the whole grove of trees around. Nothing moved. Isaak paused for a long while, his head bowed.

Then he lifted his face, now shining with the tears of his grief, and he said, very simply: "Sail on. Sail on in peace, my father, my friends… Amen."

Chapter Thirteen

The Cloud Lightens

The next few days were very difficult for everyone. Day after day, and night after night, the cloud of grief hung heavy over each and every person. In beds, in huts, around the fire, the empty spaces left by those who were no longer there felt, at every moment, like great gaps and holes in their lives. It was so hard to get beyond that sense of absolute loss; of blank emptiness.

Both Isaak and Liesa felt the loss of their fathers with deep pain. All his life, Isaak's father had been like a beacon to him; a constant light that was steady and always there. Likewise for Liesa, her father had been like an ever-present warm glow for her: always loving, always gentle. Now the light of each was gone, gone forever.

Isaak could not bear to be alone in his father's hut. Mara, Oupa Andries and Liesa were grieving for Gert themselves, but Mara's heart was moved by Isaak's pain too. So she took Isaak in. After all, they had all loved the skipper too, and Isaak had loved Gert. It seemed right. And, somehow, the grief that they shared helped them all to feel for each other. Although the bleakness and the emptiness were still there, the sharp, painful edges of their grief slowly softened. Gradually, day after slow day, they began to lift their heads and look about them.

What had happened for Isaak, Liesa, Mara and Oupa Andries also happened for many others in that small, tight-knit community. Their ability to feel for each other, and to share their grief, sent a slow but gradual breath of healing through the whole group. But as other heads began to lift from the worst of their personal losses, a new, stark awareness grew beside it. The total loss of their fishing boat and the fishermen – apart from Jantjie and Isaak there were no more able-bodied men in the community – meant that they were stranded. How were they now to survive at the cove?

Braam and Senzo had been amazing over those dark days. People had barely been able to notice, but they had quietly got on with collecting water and firewood, gathering what they could from the rocks and the gardens, and making fire and food for everyone. But supplies were now really low. The food that Isaak had brought was used up, and there was now very little left over for anyone to eat.

Fortunately, Isaak had brought some extra money with him. It was not a lot. He had planned, when he left, to give it as a parting gift to his father to use on the Malgas. Most of the people who had lost husbands, fathers or sons were still too grief-stricken to face the village just yet. Braam and Senzo said they'd go, but they needed someone to show them which shops to go to. They didn't know Plettenberg Bay. So Mara agreed to go. She knew best what supplies they needed anyway. As soon as possible they set off to buy the most urgently needed supplies.

The money did not go far, however, and they were able to bring little back with them. They knew that it was now urgent to catch something as well. So Isaak, Braam, Senzo, and Jantjie took the four rods to the rocks to try to bring in some fish as well.

It felt so wrong for Isaak to be holding the rod that he'd given to his father. At first, he didn't want to use it. He gave it to Braam to use.

Braam hesitated, and then he asked: "What do you think the skipper would *really* have wanted, Isaak? Don't you think he would have wanted you to enjoy this rod – just as he did?" He added: "Besides, Isaak, you're the best fisherman among us. The skipper would have wanted a *good* fisherman to use this rod – someone who can bring in some fish, not someone like me who has hardly fished at all. Heirso, Isaak, jy moet dit gebruik."

Isaak thought for a while. He remembered his father's delight on Christmas morning, and the fun he'd had on the rocks with Gert. "You're right, Braam. Of course you're right," he admitted. And, at last, Isaak smiled; the first smile for what had seemed like years.

Senzo was the only one who had not used a fishing rod before. Braam and Jantjie, although they hadn't had much experience, at least knew the basics. So Isaak started by teaching Senzo to cast. He showed him with his own rod first, explaining what he was doing. Then he asked him to try a cast. Senzo gave his rod a mighty heave and his sinker crashed into the water, almost at his feet.

Senzo's face was a picture. He couldn't believe he could make such a mess of it. "Not a bad beginning, Senzo – at least it didn't hit your ear!" laughed Braam.

Then Senzo laughed, and finally, Isaak and Jantjie did too. It felt so good to be able to let go at last. And as he laughed, Isaak knew his father would have wanted this too. He felt so much better for it. He remembered him once saying, "Whatever happens, Isaak, it's not so bad that you can't pick yourself up again – and a laugh is the very best way of starting."

When they caught their breath again, Isaak said, "Try holding the rod more lightly, Senzo, and don't heave so hard. Let the rod do the work."

So Senzo tried again, and this time it was much better. Soon he was really getting the hang of it. Isaak then showed him how to bait up a hook, and he explained how to strike when there was a good strong bite on the line, not for every little nibble.

By the end of the lesson, both Braam and Jantjie had brought in a fish each. They were on the bite today, so Isaak was keen to start himself. They really needed a good haul to feed everyone. It was not long before Isaak caught his first: a good-sized fish. And by the end of the day they had, between them, caught enough for a decent supper for everyone. Even Senzo had managed to catch a little one!

More important than anything, however, they all *felt* so much better. For Isaak and Jantjie especially, the laugh, as well as getting out and doing something active, had really helped. They were all able to bring not only food to the huts, but also a new mood: the first feeling of a new beginning.

The next day, at last, the women, children and older people also felt able to go out together to gather shell fish. And again, they not only brought in food, but they also felt better for it. Liesa had gone diving. She'd brought up a good haul of perlemoen and alikreukels, as well as a few kreef. But the best moment had been when she'd got a seekat stuck all over her arm, and this time she had not been able to shake it off. There were squeals and shrieks from the women and children, and delighted laughter when she finally shook it loose. That moment was a tonic for them all.

With more fish the young men brought in that day, as well as what the others had collected, they all had a good meal that evening. The mood round the fire, as they sat all together, was lighter. At last the heavy cloud of grief was beginning to lift. But Mara, more than anyone, knew that things had to be talked about, and perhaps now was the time.

"Mense," she said, "I know it's difficult, but we must talk. We all know that things can't stay as they are for long. The money has now been used up. The few supplies we bought may last a while, but they *will* run out – and quite soon."

She paused. "Isaak, I'm sure, will stay on here as long as he's needed. But Braam and Senzo must go back to Knysna soon to take up their jobs again. The problem is that we can't all live off what we can gather off the rocks and in the gullies – and the few fish that Isaak and Jantjie alone can bring in. It just will not... "

Braam interrupted. "Sorry, Mara, but I've got to say this. It's not only our jobs, it's Isaak's job too."

Isaak waved this aside. "No!" he said. "I must be here. This is where I belong. I must stay to help here."

But Braam ignored him and continued, "And then there's the group. Without Isaak, his guitar playing, and his lead in the singing, the group will just fold."

Senzo nodded his head at this. Then he added, "You can't do much good for your people here by catching a few fish, Isaak. You can do much more by coming back to Knysna. There, at least you can earn money to help where it's needed."

Several heads round the fire nodded at this. Then Mara broke in again. She was well known for saying exactly what she thought, and that's what she did now.

"Ek verstaan, and I agree with Braam and Senzo," she said. "Nou hoor vir my, Isaak. You and my daughter Liesa love one another. You know that. We all know that. It's now time that you young people get married and make a life for yourselves – and you can't do that here."

Liesa was embarrassed. "Ag, Ma!" she exclaimed and buried her head in her arms. There was a chuckle round the circle. But her mother had not finished yet. "We are tough people here, Isaak. You should know that. We can look after ourselves: we can start again somewhere else."

"Dis waar," called out someone else. "Of course we can. We all have relatives or friends in Plettenberg Bay, Kranshoek – or even in Knysna. They'll help us make a start."

"And we're not so useless that we can't work still," called out another.

Poor Isaak looked ashamed. He hung his head.

Jantjie's mother came up to him and gently put her hand on his arm. "It's alright, Isaak," she said, "We know you mean well. We know how much you've already done for us – me, more than anyone. But Mara's right. All we want is for you and Liesa to have a chance to start your own life. What people have been saying is that we can look after ourselves, and you don't have to worry – that's all."

Isaak slowly lifted his head, and then put his arms around her. A warm cheer went round the group.

"Kom, Isaak. Sing vir ons. Dis wat ons graag wil hê," called someone.

"Yes, that's what we *really* need from you, Isaak," called another.

So he fetched the guitar, and gathered Braam and Senzo behind him. Without saying a word, they knew what they were going to do: they knew what was needed, and what was wanted, at that moment. Isaak struck a clear chord and they broke into a song that had often been sung around the fire before: a song that Isaak's father had played, a song that everyone knew and loved. In no time, it was no longer their three voices alone, but the voices of all around the fire that wove and lifted into the night.

Yes, things *were* going to be alright. They could do it, they knew.

Chapter Fourteen

The Call of the Fish Eagle

After more discussion that night, everyone had decided that they'd all leave together the day after next; at the same time as Isaak, Braam and Senzo. Nobody wanted to leave the cove, their home for so long. But it was just not possible to stay. They couldn't afford a new boat, and they didn't have enough men to sail it, even if they could. They simply could not survive there any longer. A new start *had* to be made, and the sooner the better.

The last day at the cove dawned windy and blustery, but still clear. People were busy collecting up, cleaning, and packing the few things that they needed to take with them.

Although Isaak also had much to do, he went in search of Liesa. He wanted to visit the site of the wreck for one last time. He felt he could cope with it now, and somehow he knew that this was the place to bid his final farewell to his father and the fishermen. But he wanted to do it with Liesa; that is, if she felt the same way about it.

Isaak did not have to look far. Liesa had already done the washing and was hanging things up to dry, including her new dress. For Liesa, nothing would be packed up that was dirty!

He helped her hang up the last few things, and then asked her if she would come with him. "I'm sorry to ask this of you, Liesa. But... it's just that I really want us to do this together, if you want it too."

Liesa smiled, and put her hand gently on his cheek. "Ja, Isaak. Graag. I do want to be with you, and I'd like to be there for my father too."

In the fierce, blustery wind, Isaak and Liesa picked their way carefully over the rocks. The wind had whipped up the waves, and flying spray and foam stung their eyes, but Isaak recognised the place: he would never forget it. He took Liesa's hand and together they stood, facing the angry sea, the jagged, black rocks, and the wind that buffeted and roared around their ears. A picture, and something of the feeling, of what it must have been like for the men on the Malgas formed in their minds: the sheer, blinding terror of it. Liesa covered her eyes and her lips moved: Isaak held her, knowing what must be in her mind at that moment.

Then suddenly, Isaak gripped Liesa's hand hard – so hard it hurt. His eyes were staring, and he was leaning forward into the wind, as if listening. Then, slowly, his grip relaxed. There were tears in his eyes, but also, a peaceful look had descended on his face. He turned to her and led her back. The roar and rush of the wind was too loud in their ears to talk.

When they reached the shelter of the trees near the boat house, Liesa stopped and looked at him. He still had a faraway look in his eyes. "What was it, Isaak?" she asked gently.

He looked at her, and slowly his eyes came back from wherever they'd been. "It was... it was so strange, Liesa. I don't know if you can believe this, but I... I heard him. I really heard my father calling in the roar of the wind and those waves."

He looked down, and seemed to be hearing it in his mind once more. Then, again, he looked up into Liesa's eyes. "He was calling to me – but not for help. He was saying 'Follow it, Isaak, *always* follow it'."

"I believe you, Isaak. Of course I believe you," said Liesa, pressing his hand. "But, but what did he mean?"

"Do you remember after that dream – I said I'd speak to him again. Well I did, and he was very clear about it. He didn't want me back on the Malgas. He said I could do more by following the music. And he ended with those words: 'Follow it, Isaak, always follow it.' I remember it so clearly. And, now, there he was, saying it again."

Liesa smiled. "And you will. I know you will," she said. "Come, perhaps you should tell him so." And she led him to the edge of the grave under the boat house.

They both stood silently, their heads bowed. Then lifting his eyes, Isaak said simply, "I will, Pa. Don't worry, I will."

Slowly the two of them walked away from the grave, over the dunes, and sat on the sand at the edge of the river, looking up towards the forest. It was quieter than on the shore, but the wind still gusted around them, stinging their legs with sand.

Liesa leaned her head against his chest. "Isaak, come with me to the rocky shelf – just this last time," she whispered.

So they waded across the river and made their way up to the shelf. As usual, the wind was not blowing here and the sun was still warm. Again, without the need of words, they stripped their clothes off and dived into the clear, golden, softness of the water. Like a pair of otters, they swam, circled and dived, touched and rolled, until laughing and dripping, they pulled themselves back up onto the shelf and lay back on its warmth. They lay there quietly for a while, enjoying the sun on their skin, and the feeling of contentment that glowed and warmed them from the inside.

Then slowly, deliberately, Liesa rolled over until the length of her body lay stretched out against his. She took his head in her hands and kissed him long and gently. And it was she, this time, who said, "Isaak, ek het jou lief. Ek het jou *so* lief."

Isaak's eyes sparkled. "And I love you too, Liesa. I love you *so* much that I want you to marry me. Will you, Liesa? Will you? I want you for ever, and ever, and ever!"

Liesa rolled in his arms and laughed and cried, all together. "Oh, yes!" she finally got out. "Yes, Isaak! Yes! Yes! Yes! Let's make it soon!"

So they planned their wedding – and it *would* be soon: soon after they got to Knysna.

"And... and perhaps, Liesa, you could join the group. It would be great to sing with you. Your voice is *so* clear and beautiful! Wat dink jy daarvan?" asked Isaak excitedly.

There was just so much to talk about now. But it was already past midday, and there was still a great deal for them both to get done before the next day. So, for the last time, Isaak and Liesa made their way back down the river.

As they got back to the huts, the first thing they did was to look for Mara. Liesa was bursting to tell her mother the news. They found her digging up her wilde knoffel bulbs in the garden: she was not going to leave these behind!

When Liesa told her that they'd decided to get married and start their life together in Knysna, she wrapped her daughter in her arms with happiness. "Ag, my Liesa! My Liesa! That's just the best thing I could hear!"

She turned to Isaak who was standing back, a little nervously. "There, you see, I knew you'd do it," she laughed. "Come here, and give your new Ma a hug!" So he did. And, laughing with happiness, the three of them danced around the knoffel patch.

Then, asking Liesa to wait for just a moment, Mara beckoned for Isaak to come inside the hut. She dug around in a box in the corner and then she came forward holding something in her hand. She opened her hand, and there, nestled in her palm was a beautiful, simple gold ring. "Isaak, as jy van hierdie ring hou, is dit joune. It was my own mother's, and I've always kept it safe for just this day. But only if you like it, you understand."

Immediately, Isaak knew that Liesa would love it. But more than that, he knew it would mean just so much to her.

"Dis pragtig, really beautiful," he said, touching it lightly with his finger. "Dankie, Ma. I know what this will mean to Liesa."

As usual, the news spread fast in the little community. That evening, as they gathered around the fire, there was an expectant hush. Mara stood up. She looked at the small group of faces around her: the people she had known all her life.

"Tomorrow, we must leave the cove and find new homes and work where we can," she said. "It will hurt us all to have to leave each other and this place, our Covie that has been our home for so long." Then her tough, wrinkled face broke into a broad smile. "But the good news is we don't have to part just yet." She turned to Liesa and then to Isaak. "My Liesa, and young Isaak here are to be married in Knysna. They want the wedding in just three weeks from now. And everyone is invited: every single one of you!"

Calls rang out from all sides.

"Ons seënwense, Isaak and Liesa!"

"Veels geluk! Alles van die beste, julle twee!"

"Ons sal vir seker daar wees!"

Then Isaak drew Liesa forward to the front of the group.

"One last thing tonight," he said. He took Liesa's hand and, slipping the ring on her finger, smiled at her and said, "Let this be the promise of my love for you, for ever and ever, my Liesa."

Her eyes were wide, delighted but surprised. "But... where...?" And before she could say any more, Isaak sealed her lips with a kiss. "Tell you later," he whispered.

A great cheer rang out from the group. "The Lord bless you both!" they called. And everyone gathered around to kiss them, to hug them, and to wish them well in their life together.

So, instead of sadness that last night, there was excitement and much talk about the wedding: where it would be in Knysna, how to get there, who to stay with, and most of all, just the happiness that everyone felt for Isaak and Liesa for their new beginning. Also, because they knew that they'd be seeing one another again in a short time, it gave everyone a purpose too. It would be good to come together with news of a positive start. Each person left that evening with added hope and determination.

The next morning, however, was not so easy. Early on, with one mind, they'd gathered together below the boat house. This was really the moment when they would stand together at the cove, their beloved Covie, for the last time: the moment when they would say their final farewell to their men. They stood together in silence, some holding hands, some standing alone, but all bonded by one feeling. In silence, they felt it and shared it. Then, tears streaming down many a face, they walked quietly up to the huts, picked up their belongings and started their journey up the steep hill.

Isaak and Liesa were among the last to leave. As they climbed up the hill behind Mara, there was a clear call high on the wind above them, 'Kuy-yoo kya kya kya'.

They both stopped and looked up.

Its chest white against the blue of the sky, the fish eagle was circling directly above. It seemed to look down at them. And then, again, it cried, 'Kuy-yoo kya kya kya'.

Isaak raised his arm. "Stay well, my friend," he called. "Veilig bly."

Turning, he took Liesa's hand, and they bent their backs into getting their loads up the hill.

Postscript

This story is based on truth. In the first half of the twentieth century, a small fishing community *did* live at the little cove that is described in this story, long known as 'Covie'.

The history of this specific community has not been formally recorded. However, it is known that they were Griquas. They were direct or indirect descendents of the great and tragic Griqua trek of the 18th and 19th centuries. Under the leadership of Abraham Le Fleur, a group of Griquas, who had been displaced from their land by the British in East Griqualand, trekked all the way from Kokstad to settle at Kranshoek in the early years of the 20th century.[1] Some of this group moved from Kranshoek to form a fishing community at the mouth of the Salt River in the early part of the last century.[2] This information is supported by remembered family names and oral accounts of what happened.[3]

At the time of the story, the original Griqua language had largely been lost, and most people in the community spoke a colloquial form of Afrikaans. To capture the flavour and feel of their language, some of the direct speech in the story reflects its idiomatic usage. Christian belief and a tradition of group singing was strong in this community.

The cove itself, with its river, still exists. The indigenous forest that surrounds it has, fortunately, not been devastated by woodcutters. It is now a nature reserve, and is still wild

Postscript

and isolated. As in the old days, there is no road to the cove, the only access being on foot.

The community lived in a clearing in the forest a short way above the cove. This clearing is still just visible. The boat house, which was situated in a grove of trees just above the beach, stood for a long time after the community left, until it eventually rotted and was removed. The site of the boat house is also still visible, if you look carefully. The fishermen's grave may, or may not, have been under the boat house: this is not known.

The fishing community's boat *was* indeed wrecked, and as described, all the fishermen but one were lost. Without the boat, and with all those men lost, the small community could not survive. They had to leave the cove and start anew elsewhere.

The devastation of large areas of the indigenous forests around Knysna *did* occur, and it was only when sufficient awareness of conservation issues grew, in that community and more widely in the country, that the destruction was somewhat curtailed.

The actual characters in the story and their relationships are fictional, but perhaps there really were people such as Isaak, the skipper, Liesa and the others. And perhaps their spirits do still inhabit the cove, its river, and its forest? Who knows? The fish eagle – or at least its descendents – certainly do.

1. Pinnock, Don: "The Trek to Nomansland". *Getaway*, November 2006.
2. Storrar, Patricia: *Portrait of Plettenberg Bay*. Centaur, Cape Town, 1978.
3. Chief Samuel Jansen, Kranshoek.

Glossary of Afrikaans and Colloquial Language

Ag, dis sommer twak! – Oh, this is just nonsense!
Ag, ek gee nie om nie – Oh, I don't care
Ag, ek weet glad nie – Oh, I just don't know
As jy van hierdie ring hou, is dit joune – If you like the ring, it's yours
Blikkitaar – Simple guitar made with a rectangular empty tin as the body or resonator, meaning 'tin guitar'
Boet – Affectionate term for brother
Braai – Cook over hot coals
Daai twee – Those two
Daar's hy, kant en klaar – That's it, finished and done
Dalk is daar moeilikheid! – Perhaps there's trouble!
Dankie, Oom! Baie, baie dankie – Thank you, sir! Thank you very, very much
Deurmekaar – Mixed up
Die Here sy dank – Praise be to God
Die Vissers' Lied – The Fishermen's Song
Dis in die bloed – It's in the bloodline
Dis my eerste, my heel eerste nuwe rok – It's my first, my very first new dress
Dis pragtig – It's beautiful
Dis sommer twak – That's just nonsense
Dis vreeslik – That's dreadful
Dis waar - It's true
Droëvis – Dried fish

Glossary

Ek beloof julle – I promise you all
Ek gee nie om nie – I don't care
Ek het jou lief – I love you
Ek hou van jou – I like you
Ek verstaan – I understand
Ek weet nie – I don't know
Ek's bang, *so* bang – I'm scared, *so* scared
Ek's nog nie seker nie – I don't know yet
Ek's *so* jammer – I'm *so* sorry
Ek stem saam – I agree
Ek't gesê 'seil op', en dit beteken seil op *nou!* – I said 'up sail', and that means up sail *now*!
En toe? – And so?
En... wat is *dit*? – And... what is *this*?
Gou maak! – Quick!
Haai, wat gaan daar aan! – Hey, what's going on there!
Hier's 'n oudtjie – Here's a little chap
Hierso – Here you are
Hoe lyk *dit* dan, gaffelman! – How's *that* then, gaff-man!
Hou vas, manne! – Hold tight, men!
Ja, ek ook – Yes, me too
Ja, graag – Yes, of course
Sjoe! Hier's 'n knewel – Wow! Here's a monster
Jou slang! – You snake!
Jy moet dit gebruik – You must use it
Jy moet nou hierdie mooi dogter van jou goed dop hou! – You must now keep a sharp eye on this pretty daughter of yours!
Jy's die beste! – You're the best!
Jy's hier! Jy's nou veilig! – You're here! You're safe now!
Jy's 'n prentjie in daai rok! – You're a picture in that dress!
Jy weet dit mos – You know that well
Kalander – Outeniqua Yellowwood
Kap hom weg! – Cut it away!

Kierie – wooden club
Klink 'n bietjie beter – Sounds a bit better
Kom my eie Liesa – Come my own Liesa
Kom my mooiding – Come my beauty
Kom ons sing vir hulle 'n stukkie – Come, let's sing them a piece
Kom saam – Come with us
Kom, gou-gou! – Come, hurry!
Kragtig – Powerful
Kreef – Crayfish
Kyk daar! Die vis loop vandag – Look there! The fish are on the move today
Kyk hier – Look here
Laat ons bid – Let us pray
Laat ons dank betuig – Let us offer thanks
Laat waai! – Get a move on!
Lied van die Bos – Song of the Forest
Liegbek – Liar
Los my uit – Leave me alone
Luisakke – Lazybones
Lyne op, en span die seil! Gou-gou! Roer julle! – Lines up, and set the sail! Quick! Move now!
Ma – Mother
Maak gou – Hurry
Maak vir ons musiek – Give us some music
Maar Liesa, luister tog na my – But Liesa, please listen to me
Maar tog die wenner – But still the winner
Maar wie weet – But who knows
Malgas – Gannet
Meneer – Mister; sir
Mense – People
Moenie laf wees nie – Don't be silly
Môre – Short for 'good morning'

Glossary

Môre is Kersdag – Tomorrow is Christmas day
Môre's nog 'n dag, boet – Tomorrow's another day, brother
My seun – My son
Nee, nee. Kan jy nie sien nie? – No. No. Can't you see?
Net om dankie te sê, ou maat – Just a small thank you, old friend
Nie nou nie – Not now
Niks – Nothing
Nog! Nog! – More! More!
Nooit! Dit was myne! – Never! It was mine!
Nou hoor vir my – Now you listen to me
Nou ja? – Well then?
Nou toe nou. Net betyds vir die visbraai, nè Pa – Well, what about that. Just in time for the fish braai, not so, Dad
O dis wonderlik! – Oh it's wonderful!
Ons sal vir seeker daar wees! – We'll certainly be there!
Ons seënwense – Our blessings
Oom – Uncle; term of respect for an older man
Opskud nou – Hurry up
Pa – Father; Dad
Patats – Sweet potatoes
Potjie – Metal pot for cooking stews on an open fire
Reg, seil op, manne – Right, up sail, men
Roer jou boude! – Move your backside!
Seekat – Octopus
Skelm – Rogue
Skipper – Captain (pronounced like English 'pip', together with a rolled 'r')
Skoert! – Push off!
Skollie – Robber; gangster
Swem nou saam met my – Swim with me now
Toe nou, toe nou, my Liesatjie – There, there, my little

    Liesa
Van kleins af – Since we were little
Vat 'n dop, man – Have a drink, man
Veels geluk! Alles van die beste, julle twee! – Good luck! Everything of the best, you two!
Veilig bly – Stay safe
Verbrande Frik! – Darned Frik!
Vergeet daarvan. Nie met 'n kriewel soos dit nie! – Forget it. Not with a shrimp like this one!
Vetkoek – Rich bread roll, literally 'fat cake'
Wag net! – Just you wait!
Wat dink julle? – What do you think?
Wat dink jy daarvan? – What would you think of that?
Wat gaan in jou kop aan? – What's going on in your head?
Wat makeer, my kleintjie? – What's wrong, my little one?
Wat's als in jou sak... klippe? – What've you got in your bag... rocks?
Weet glad nie – Just don't know; wouldn't have a clue
Wilde knoffel – Wild garlic

Other teen titles by Jacana

The Story of Lucky Simelane
by Robin Malan

Lucky Fish!
by Reviva Schermbrucker

Sharp Sharp Zulu Dog
by Anton Ferreira